# Real Kids, Real Play

by Alice Zsembery

**REMINDER**
This book comes with **free** printables to
complement the activities.
Head to **www.realkidsrealplay.com.au/bookresources/**
to download.

Published by Jack and Lu's Pty Ltd

I would like to thank my darling husband, Nick, for having faith in me even when I didn't have it in myself. You have worked your butt off to ensure that we keep our patch of dirt whilst I pursue my dream. I love you always xx

To my beautiful children who played endlessly to test every activity and make this book happen. Life must've been tough(!) You two rugrats are my world.

To my brother who put up with my indecision and changes in direction. You deserve a medal. We may not always see eye to eye but we will always have each other's backs.

To my girlfriends, you know who you are. You have listened to my harebrained ideas, volunteered your children for photos, always given me the confidence to keep moving forward and empowered me to make this happen. I am honoured to be surrounded by such intelligent and inspirational women. Your support has truly made this happen. This is only the first step, so expect many more brainstorming sessions. I'll bring the wine.

To my grandparents: Grandma, Poppy and Jack. I miss you all dearly. Hopefully you are watching down with a drink in your hands as proud as punch.

To my remaining grandparent, Lu. A working mother long before that was the thing to do. You are an inspirational lady to all your daughters and grandchildren and we love you dearly. Wongabeena days may now be gone but the childhood that we had there will always stay with us. I couldn't think of a more worthy person and place in time to name my business after.

To my beautiful Dad; My number one supporter and now my angel. 10 years on and I miss you even more. Thankyou for always believing in me and I hope that you are looking down beaming with pride. Love Bags

And finally, to me. Because too infrequently do parents and carers stop to pat themselves on the back and remind themselves that they are doing a great job.

**Published by Jack & Lu's Pty Ltd**
**www.jackandlus.com**
**2nd ed.**

**First edition published by Alice Zsembery trading as Jack and Lu's in 2017.**
**This edition published by Jack & Lu's Pty Ltd in 2019.**
**Copyright © 2017 Alice Zsembery. All rights reserved.**

**For more information or enquiries email info@jackandlus.com**

**ISBN 978-0-6482123-3-1**
**Photography: Georgia Tossol, Alice Zsembery, Lynda Kinkade, Canva Stock Media**
**Logo design: Simon Liversidge**
**Featuring: Thomas, Emily, Caitlin, Patrick, Jack, Hugo, Piper, Hannah and Georgia**
**Thanks also to Treena. You can take the teacher out of the classroom, but you cannot take the classroom out of the teacher.**

Particular thanks must go to my own Mum; the strongest woman that I know and without whom, my world would stop turning.

# PREFACE

I am not a child expert. I am neither a qualified educator nor a childcare play therapist. I am just a tired, working mum who wants to give my children the best start in life but has often felt completely overwhelmed.

On a good day, I may have enough creativity to help make crafts out of an old egg carton. But on a not-so-optimal day (or let's face it, most days) I cannot even find enough creativity to dress myself beyond the clean items in the washing basket that haven't made it back into the wardrobe, let alone devise and plan an inspirational play session for my children.

I have become sick of the pressure placed on parents to sit in a playground all day, plan fun-filled activities and excursions in the hours after the kids have gone to bed, and spend copious amounts of money on toys that will only be played with for 5 minutes at best. And the clutter, oh my, the clutter in spaces I didn't even know existed!

Don't get me wrong, my kids love the outdoors and I try to get out there at every opportunity I can.

**BUT DO YOU KNOW WHAT? Some days it's raining or too hot or there's no outdoor space available or you have a younger child asleep or you can't handle the thought of putting on clothes or, hell, some days you just simply need to get stuff done around the home!**

This book is for that Mum. If you are the ethereal mum that I wished I was for so long - with endless time, money, toys (and space for the toys) and boundless creative ideas - go you. You rock my world and you are doing a fabulous job. That said, this book may not be your thing.

We all want to be the best parent that we can be and provide our mostly beautiful, sometimes challenging and always energetic children with the best opportunities in life.

We are all doing a wonderful job of raising our children with the resources that we have available. **This book is designed to make that job a little bit easier and more enjoyable.**

Some items in this book may be familiar, from a childhood long ago, some may educate you (checkout some of the preschool science experiments) and some may seem really, (like REALLY) simple. No apologies there.

My aim was to find, test and modify activities that could be done at home with everyday items. These activities are a tried-and-true list from myself and close friends

The simple criteria that each activity must fulfill to make it into this book are:

1. They must only use items commonly found around the home. Not a Betty Crocker household, but an I-haven't-been-shopping-in-3-weeks household. However, there is one exception. Balloons. Balloons never last more than 10 minutes in our household, so they always need to be bought.

2. They must not take more than 5 minutes max to set up. Unless, of course, they provide a guaranteed 10 hours' worth of entertainment. Then I would make an exception.

3. They must hold my children's attention for a much longer period than it took to set them up. For Miss 2, that's not too hard. For Master 4, on the other hand...

4. They must be accompanied by photos so that kids can choose something that they find interesting. I figure, if they choose it, they are more likely to get involved, right?

5. Words must be kept to a minimum. As a working mum who spends a significant amount of my (paid) working days in front of a computer, I don't need anything else to read. If it can't be shown in a picture, forget it.

This is something that has been 2 years in the making, and I dearly hope that it can help make every parent, guardian, grandparent's and carer's role just that little bit easier.

Now to invent something that automatically hangs out the washing...

Mum fist pumps,

*Ali*

*Mum to Master Destroyer (4 years) and Miss Independent (2 years)*

"

THERE'S NO WAY
TO BE A PERFECT
MOTHER — BUT A
MILLION WAYS TO
BE A GOOD ONE

JILL CHURCHILL

# Contents

125

144

153

180

113

# Safety

Please remember that nothing is more important than the safety of your child. This book provides indicative age ranges for each activity based on general development milestones. However, you know your child better than anyone else. Please assess every activity's suitability to your individual child's needs. Please always remember the following:

- Do not ever leave a young child alone or unsupervised for any period of time. Be particularly cautious of any activities involving water.
- Ensure that small objects are kept away from young children at all times as they may pose a choking hazard.
- Ensure any materials that may come in contact with a child are non-toxic and approved for child use.

Whilst we have made every effort to ensure that the information in this book is accurate and suggested activities are safe and workable with an adult properly supervising, we disclaim all liability for any unintended, unforeseen or improper application of the suggestions featured in this book.

# THE BASIS OF PLAY

# CHAPTER ONE

# So what is play?

Play has been described in many different ways but the common characteristics include:

- **Pleasurable**–play is an enjoyable and pleasurable activity. Play sometimes includes frustrations, challenges and fears; however, enjoyment is a key feature
- **Symbolic**–play is often pretend, it has a 'what if?' quality. The play has meaning to the player that is often not evident to the educator
- **Active**–play requires action, either physical, verbal or mental engagement with materials, people, ideas or the environment
- **Voluntary**–play is freely chosen. However, players can also be invited or prompted to play
- **Process oriented**–play is a means unto itself and players may not have an end or goal in sight
- **Self motivating**–play is considered its own reward to the player

*From Shipley's Empowering Children: Play-Based Curriculum for Lifelong Learning (2008)*

Play-based learning is described in the Australian Early Years Learning Framework as 'a context for learning through which children organise and make sense of their social worlds, as they actively engage with people, objects and representations'.

## What does this mean?

In essence, play is very important to a growing mind. Whilst it may seem like a fun, harmless activity to us adults, to children, play helps them learn, develop and grow. It assists in language development, memory skills, behaviour regulation, social adjustment, negotiation skills, risk assessment and the list goes on....

What I think a lot of parents miss, however, is that **unstructured play** is considered the best type of play for young children. It allows for use of the imagination, exploration skills and creativity.

So stress less Mama or Papa, and stop enrolling your child in every class known to man. Provide incidental learning along the way by asking probing questions and providing guidance, but let them choose their own adventure both inside and outside the home.

*There are many resources available online if you are interested in reading more. My favourites include:*

- *Early Childhood Australia: http://www.earlychildhoodaustralia.org.au/*
- *The Raising Children Network: http://raisingchildren.net.au/*

The book is structured with at least one page dedicated to each activity. Key features are outlined below:

Indicative Age Range based upon the author's experience (please note that this is guidance only and the reader should make their own judgement based upon the ability of the individual child)

# JUMPING JACK

2–5 years

List of items needed

**What you need...**

- Tape

*What kid doesn't love to hop around? Simply tape lines to the floor and have them jump over them.*

Short story (as much as you need to know and nothing more!)

A great activity for burning energy, this also enhances gross-motor skills and coordination.
You can also try the following:

- Hop over each line on one leg.
- Hop backwards over them.
- Long jump: How many lines can they jump over in one go?
- Run and jump: Experiment with how much farther they can jump with a running head start.
- Balancing beam: Take the tightrope challenge and try to walk along the line, and then jump to the next one.
- Put your feet on one end: How far can you stretch and reach?

Kids love a competition. Let them try to beat their previous score or, our favourite, beat their brother/sister. Let them experiment by creating different rules. How about the teddy doing a long jump or hopping with your eyes closed?

The longer story for those that like that little bit extra...

In the Toddler Experiments, this section is replaced with a 'Kid Friendly Explanation' of the experiment.

**Handy Hint**
As an extension activity for 3-5 year olds, try putting different numbers, letters or shapes on the floor and creating rules, such as 'Hop between the L and the R' or 'Crawl backwards to the triangle'.

Handy hints to extend the activity and ensure success

# SAVE YOUR SANITY MY FAVOURITE MUM HACKS

# CHAPTER TWO

*Call them cheats, corner cutters or lifesavers. Whatever they are, if they make life a little easier, embrace them!*

# USE YOUR GARAGE

If it's pouring outside, consider using your garage or porch if you have one.

This might be the one sanity-saving trick that helps squeeze every last morsel of your child's energy out! Pull out bikes, scooters or whatever you can find, and let them loose.

For us, it's the front porch that's the winner.

# CONTAINED BATH

Baby plays with toys, toys float away from baby, baby insists on walking, crawling or lunging after toys and mum panics when baby slips. Sound familiar? Sit your baby in a washing basket filled with toys. Seriously, it works. Remember that the usual safety precautions with monitoring children in and around water still apply.

# BOX DRAWINGS

OK, I admit it. I kicked myself when I found out about this for not having thought of it before. And I wanted to make sure that others didn't miss out on this genius. Put your children inside a box (lid open of course) and let them draw to their heart's content with crayons, textas and paint (with full supervision). And there it is! That's all! Mess avoided.
You're welcome.

# KIDS RESOURCES

*There are many resources around well and beyond the children's channel on the TV, and many get them up and moving. Some of my favourites are listed below, but there are plenty of similar ones out there.*

- **Kinderling Radio** – a kids' 24-hour radio station with songs, rhymes, story time, jokes, yoga, meditation, audio books and lullabies. The best thing about this app is that there are 'mixtapes' of songs for the whole family!
- **The Learning Station** – found on YouTube, this channel is 'Healthy Music for Child's Heart, Body and Mind' with great songs for preschoolers of all ages.
- **Just Dance Kids** – found on YouTube, this selection of videos are based on the video game of the same name.
- **Cosmic Kids Yoga** – found on YouTube, this is yoga made especially for kids' designed for mindfulness and relaxation whilst taking them on a yoga adventure.
- **Debbie Doo Kids TV** – YouTube channel with fun kids songs and plenty of colour and animation.
- **HowCast.com** (hip-hop for kids) – navigate your way to the 'Hip-Hop Dance Moves for Kids', and let them enjoy these how-to-dance videos on hip-hop dance moves. This is for the older preschooler/school child.
- **Groov3dance Channel** - YouTube how-to-dance videos. This is not actually specifically for children, but the instructions are simple, the songs are fun and they are great for the older child with interest in all things dance.

# DO-IT-YOURSELF VAULT

# CHAPTER THREE

# BATH PAINT

## Recipe 1

- Baby wash
- Cornflour
- Water
- Food colouring

Mix equal portions of baby wash and cornflour together. Add water to get to a suitable consistency (not too runny or it won't stick to the tiles). Then add 1 drop of food colouring.

## Recipe 2

- Shaving cream
- Food colouring

Simply add a drop of food colouring to some shaving cream and away you go!

### Handy Hints
1. Put the mixture in an ice cube tray before adding colour. Then you can easily mix all the different colours.
2. You can avoid overcolouring by using a wooden stick to dip into the food colouring.
3. Be sure to rinse tiles as soon as you are finished.

# FINGER PAINT

## Standard

- 3 tbs sugar
- ½ tsp. salt
- ½ cup cornstarch
- 2 cups water
- Food colouring

Combine the ingredients in a small saucepan and warm it up until the mixture thickens. Let it cool, and then add in a small amount of food colouring.

## Edible

- Greek yoghurt
- Food colouring

If you'd prefer a more temporary solution that avoids sugar and salt, try adding a drop of food dye to plain Greek yoghurt!

Note: Greek yoghurt is nice and thick, so it performs better than other yoghurts. And remember, you only need a minuscule drop of food dye to get a colour

# WINDOW PAINT

## Recipe 1

- Plain flour
- Water
- Food colouring
- Dish detergent

Use equal parts of plain flour, water and dishwashing detergent. Mix together, and add a drop of food colouring.

## Recipe 2

- Washable paints
- Dish detergent
- Cornflour (optional)

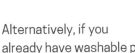

Alternatively, if you already have washable paints, just add a good squeeze of dishwashing detergent and a small amount of cornflour to thicken the mixture.

**Handy Hints**
There are plenty of recipes out there for this. The two above are tried and tested.
Or feel free to also use the bath paints instead!

# PLAYDOUGH

## Traditional

*From NMAA - Recipes For Busy Mothers*

My all-time favourite play dough recipe comes from the NMAA cookbook – a classic staple in many Australian households of the 1980s.

- ½ cup salt
- 1 cup flour
- 1 cup water
- 1 tbsp. oil
- Food colouring
- 2 tbsp. cream of tartar

Mix together the dry ingredients, and then stir in the remaining ingredients in a saucepan. Cook on medium heat for 3-5 minutes stirring until the dough comes together. Let it cool slightly, and knead it to a smooth dough. Store in an airtight container or ziplock bag.

## No Cook

*From Playschool website on abc.net.au*

Our classic kids show *Playschool* has provided us with our staple no-cook play dough. I have found this one to be the best consistency.

- 1 cup plain flour
- ¼ cup salt
- 1 tbsp. cooking oil
- Food colouring
- ½ cup water

Mix the flour and salt together in a large bowl. Make a well in the centre of the dry ingredients, and pour in the oil.
Add a few drops of food colouring to the water and mix to combine. Add the liquid –a little at a time – to the flour and oil.
Knead until the mixture is smooth and the consistency of scone dough. If the mixture is too dry, add more water. Likewise, if it's too sticky, add more flour.

# BATH BOMBS

- 1 cup Epsom salt
- 1 tbsp. baking soda
- Food colouring
- 1 ½ tbsp. lemon juice

Mix together all the ingredients, and press firmly into a cup, ramekin or something similar (it's easier if it's a flexible plastic or silicone material so that it can be 'popped' out later on). Dry overnight or in the freezer for an hour, and then press it out of the cups.
Hint: these balls 'fizzle' gently. For a more visual reaction, substitute lemon juice for citric acid (not a common household item) and add a few drops of oil to bind.

 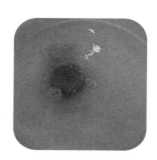

# PUFFY PAINTS

- 1 tbsp. SR flour
- 1 tbsp. salt
- A little bit of water
- Food colouring

Mix to a relatively liquid consistency. Paint it onto paper and then put it in the microwave for 30 secs so that it puffs up.
Allow it to cool before kids touch it.

# GLUE

- 1 tbsp. cornflour
- 1 tbsp. water
- 1 cup boiling water

Blend together cornflour and water until smooth. Pour boiling water over cornflour mixture, stirring constantly over heat until it thickens slightly and becomes clear.

# BEANIE BALLS

I'm sure we all made these many moons ago and have totally forgotten about them!
Grab two balloons and a funnel. Pour barley, dried beans or even flour (for a stress ball effect) into a balloon through the funnel. Tie off the filled balloon, cut the neck from a second balloon and squeeze it over the filled balloon to cover the tie .

# BUBBLE MIXTURE

There are many different bubble mixtures out there and I believe that the best utilise glycerine, which can be found at the supermarket or chemist. That said, I know we don't all keep some at home, so I have included a non-glycerine recipe too.

- 7 parts water
- 3 parts dish detergent
- 1 part glycerine

Mix all ingredients together. Let the mixture sit for a little before you use it and away you go!

- ½ cup dish detergent
- 1 cup water
- 2 tsp. sugar

Mix all ingredients together, and it's ready to go.

# CLAY

- 1 ½ cups plain flour
- ½ cup salt
- ¼ cup vegetable oil
- ½ cup water

Mix together dry ingredients.
Add water and oil a little at a time, mixing as you go. Knead for 3-4 minutes until you get clay.
NB: If the mixture is cracking, add more wet ingredients. And if it's too sticky, add more flour.

# KID-FRIENDLY SONGS

# CHAPTER FOUR

We all get sick of kids songs from time to time, and I find myself scrambling to think of tunes with children-friendly lyrics whilst not driving me around the bend!

Here is a list of songs I have compiled that I believe are suitable for children's ears. Some may simply be understood at a different level by a child than an adult! I am certain you will find something that suits your taste.

## BALLADS

*Spin your child around in your arms and belt it out!*

Let It Be – The Beatles
All You Need Is Love – The Beatles
Kokomo – The Beach Boys
Morningtown Ride – The Seekers
Somewhere Over the Rainbow/
What a Wonderful World – Israel Kamakawiwo'ole
You're Beautiful - James Blunt
Two Strong Hearts – John Farnham
The Horses – Daryl Braithwaite

(I've Had) The Time of My Life – Bill Medley & Jennifer Warnes
Just The Way You Are – Bruno Mars
I Wanna Dance With Somebody – Whitney Houston
Just The Way You Are – Billy Joel
I Just Called To Say I Love You – Stevie Wonder
Eternal Flame – The Bangles
You're the Voice – John Farnham

## POWERFUL LYRICS

*These songs may be for a slightly older audience, but they contain a beautiful message and/or powerful lyrics for kids.*

What Makes You Beautiful – One Direction
Shake It Off – Taylor Swift
Home – Phillip Phillips
Pompeii – Bastille
Try – Colbei Caillat
Hurricane – The Vamps
Try – P!nk
Pass Me By – R5
Firework – Katy Perry
Roar – Katy Perry
Royals - Lorde
Wake Me Up – Avicii

Keep Your Head Up – Andy Grammar
Brave – Sara Bareilles
Don't Stop Believin' – Journey
Walking On The Moon – The Police
Can't Stop The Feeling – Justin Timberlake
Suddenly I See – KT Tunstall
A Sky Full of Stars - Coldplay
Heal The World – Michael Jackson
Hey Soul Sister - Train
Ho Hey – The Lumineers
Pride – The Goo Goo Dolls (with Elmo)
Anything Could Happen – Ellie Goulding

## ADD YOUR OWN...

# PRE SCHOOLER DANCE PARTY

*The boppy hits to get those bodies moving...*

Octopus's Garden – The Beatles
Yellow Submarine – The Beatles
With A Little Help From My Friends – The Beatles
Twist and Shout – The Beatles
Drive My Car – The Beatles
Fixing a Hole – The Beatles
Hello Goodbye – The Beatles
Good Day Sunshine – The Beatles
Here Comes the Sun – The Beatles
Hippy Hippy Shake – The Beatles
I Saw Her Standing There- The Beatles
I Want to Hold Your Hand – The Beatles
Johnny B Goode – The Beatles
Love Me Do – The Beatles
Please Mr Postman – The Beatles
Roll Over Beethoven – The Beatles
Blue Suede Shoes – Elvis Priestley
Footloose – Kenny Loggins
I Got a Feeling – The Black Eyed Peas
YMCA – Village People
Rockin' Robin – The Jackson 5
I Like to Move It – Will.i.am
Monster Mash – Bobby Pickett
Purple People Eater – Sheb Wooley
Steal My Kisses – Ben Harper
Splish Splash – Bobby Darin
Happy – Pharrell Williams
Slice Of Heaven – Dave Dobbyn
Good Feeling – Flo Rida
Brown Eyed Girl - Van Morrison
Ain't No Mountain High Enough - Marvin Gaye & Tammi Terrell
Crazy Little Thing Called Love - Queen
We Built This City - Jefferson Starship
New Sensation - INXS
Walk The Dinosaur – Was (Not Was)
La Bamba – Ritchie Vallens
The Twist – Chubby Checker
I Should Be So Lucky – Kylie Minogue
Boom Chicka Boom - Unknown/Various
Dancing In The Street – Martha & The Vandellas
Bicycle Race – Queen
Gangnam Style – Psy

Best Day Of My Life – American Authors
Wake Me Up Before You Go Go - Wham
Ice Ice Baby – Vanilla Ice
Moves Like Jagger – Maroon 5
One Love – Bob Marley
Count On Me – Bruno Mars
1234 – Feist
What I Am – Will.I.Am
I'm Yours – Jason Mraz
Surfin' USA - Beach Boys
Dear Jessie – Madonna
Sweet Child O' Mine – Guns N' Roses
FunkyTown – Lipps Inc
I'm a Believer – Smash Mouth
Mickey – Toni Basil
Groove Is In The Heart – Dee-Lite
Opening Theme – The Monkees
Don't Stop Movin' – S Club 7
S Club Party – S Club 7
We Like To Party (The Vengabus) – Vengaboys
MMM Bop - Hanson
Everybody (Backstreet's Back) – Backstreet Boys
Celebration – Kool & The Gang
Spice Up Your life – Spice Girls
Don't Worry, Be Happy – Bob Marley
Down Under – Men at Work
Eagle Rock – Daddy Cool
Sultans Of Swing  - Dire Straits
Walk Of Life – Dire Straits
Despacito (Remix) - Luis Fonsi & Daddy Yankee Remix
It's Still Rock and Roll to Me – Billy Joel
I Love Rock 'n Roll – Joan Jett & the Blackhearts
Flashdance.. What a Feeling – Irene Cara
All Night Long (All Night) – Lionel Richie
Jump – Kriss Kross
Jump - Van Halen
Hooked on a Feeling – Blue Swede
The Way You Make Me Feel – Michael Jackson
I'll Be There for You – The Rembrandts
Everyday – Buddy Holly
Dancing On The Ceiling – Lionel Ritchie
Girls Just Want To Have Fun – Cyndi Lauper
Timber – Pitbull ft. Ke$ha

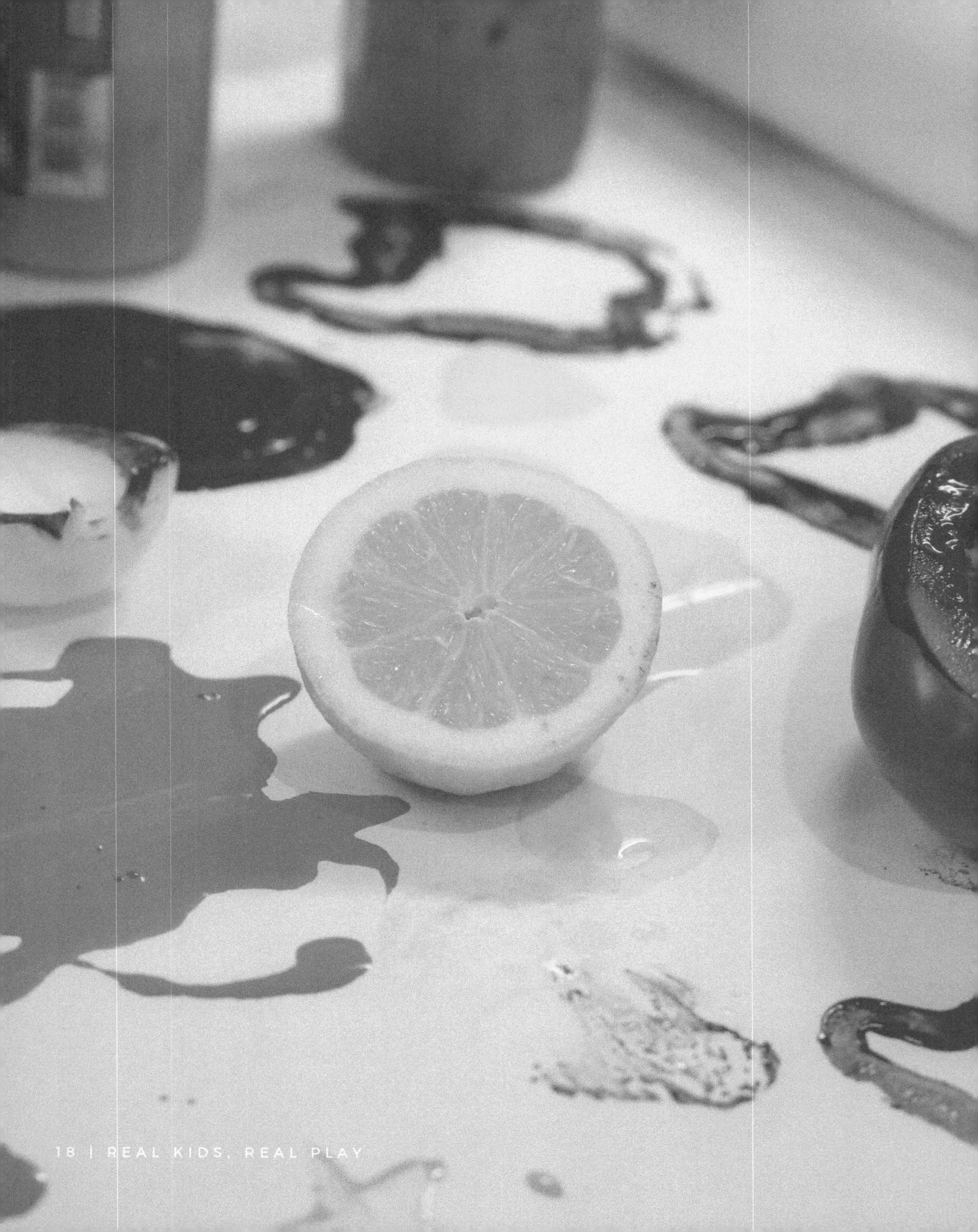

# ACTIVITIES USING HOUSEHOLD ITEMS

# CHAPTER FIVE

# "

# ENTER INTO CHILDREN'S PLAY AND YOU WILL FIND THE PLACE WHERE THEIR MINDS, HEARTS AND SOULS MEET

**VIRGINIA AXLINE**

# TWINKLE TWINKLE LITTLE STAR

*Grab a large box, pop some holes in the top and poke your Christmas lights through it for a magical experience.*

**Handy Hint**
Once your littlie is learning to crawl, this makes for a wonderful tunnel for them.

This activity is a feast of the senses for a younger child. Make sure that the box remains open at both ends and that the roof is out of full arm's reach from the child. Full supervision is required, but your little one will love the sparkles above them.
**Note: Be sure to always keep cord out of reach and turn off lights when not in use.**

**What you need...**

- Christmas lights
- Large cardboard box

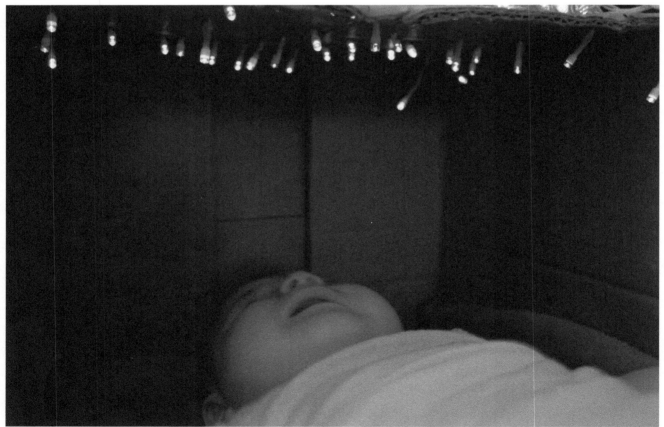

# FINGER PUPPETS

*Grab some finger puppets, and slowly move them in front of your baby's face, making conversation along the way.*

**Handy Hint**

Finger puppets can be picked up cheaply online or at your favourite Swedish chain store. However, if you are looking for a quick solution, go ahead and cut the ends from a rubber glove, grab a marker and decorate it to your heart's content. Or you could even decorate some peanut shells (provided that they are kept well away from baby)! This is the perfect activity to involve an older child in.

This activity is perfect for babies aged 1-3 months as their eyesight is improving and they are constantly observing the world around them. Be sure to move slowly with the puppets to help them keep track of them. Introduce the puppets, and make funny voices for them.

Younger babies particularly respond well to patterns (more so than colours). So if you are making them yourself, be sure to include some patterns like stripes, dots and chevrons.

**What you need...**

- Finger puppets
OR
- Dishwashing glove

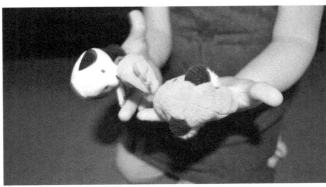

# PAPER CRUMPLE

*Allow your baby to play with crumpled paper. Simple.*

**Handy Hint**
Be sure to constantly watch your baby to prevent them from putting paper in their mouth. Be particularly mindful of coloured paper; once it gets soggy, it can be very difficult to get the colours off your baby's skin!

As your baby's auditory and motor skills are increasing at around 1-3 months, a piece of paper becomes the perfect item to explore. Seriously, you wouldn't believe how much babies like this simple item! I like to start off by crumpling the paper behind the baby's head, and allowing them time to register the noise and attempt to figure out which direction it is coming from. For older babies, allow the baby to hold the paper in their hand and explore the crumpled piece. It is also great to provide them with slightly different materials - tissue paper works really well, as does gift-wrapping paper (as it has some interesting prints).

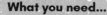

**What you need...**

Paper

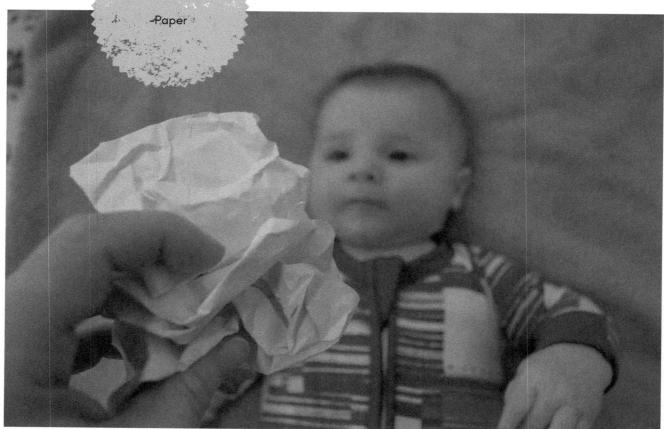

# UP UP AND AWAY

*Sit on the floor in front of your baby. Carefully lift them up in the air and then slowly roll onto your back and allow them to 'fly' over your head.*

**Handy Hint**
If it's easier, place your baby on your shins, lie backwards and gently raise your legs.

**What you need...**

- Nothing!

This activity works well for babies 3 months and up as their gross motor skills are improving. Babies will enjoy the feeling of 'flying'. And even though you are fully supporting them, it helps develop the muscles in their back and shoulders, particularly when they lift their head up. The flying motion will also help them experience their centre of gravity shifting.

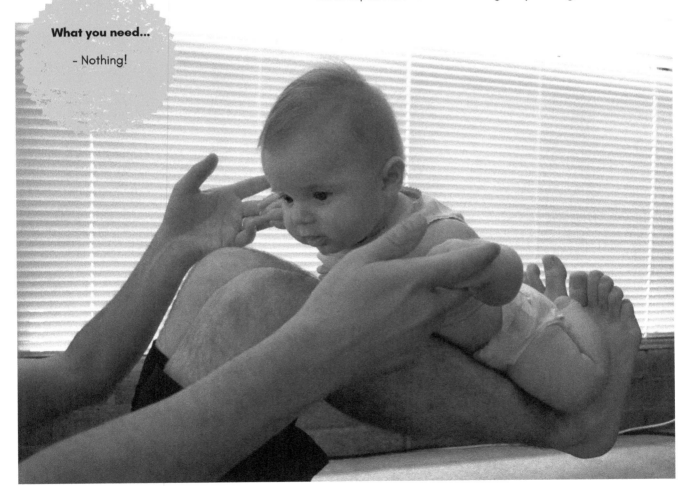

# SENSORY HOOP

*Grab a hula hoop, and wrap some scarves or other items around it that have different textures. Place your baby in the middle on their tummy, and let them explore.*

**Handy Hint**
Clip on some of your baby's pram toys to the hoop for extra stimulation

**What you need...**
- Hula hoop
- Sensory items such as scarves, a lei, pom poms or a ribbon

This activity is great for babies 3-6 months old as they are getting better at tummy time and their neck muscles are strengthening. We often forget to provide babies with sensory experiences for their feet as well, but the nature of this activity allows them to extend their legs and feel textures on their feet. **Be sure to maintain constant supervision of your baby and securely wrap any ribbon or other potentially hazardous items.**

# DIY HANGING MOBILE

*Hang a piece of rope across your baby's cot, making sure it is secure and tight and fully out of their reach. Use large pegs or binder clips to peg a variety of items to the line, like small, soft toys, a sock, a picture of someone etc.*

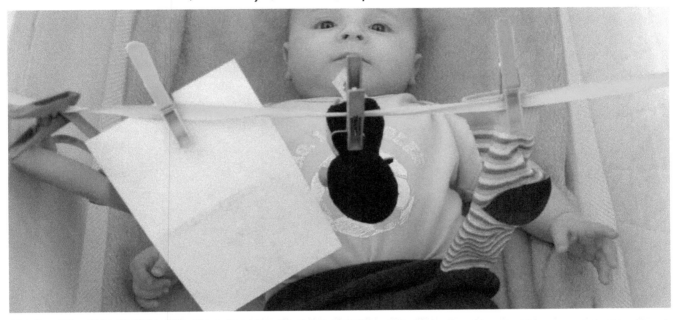

**Handy Hint**
**Your baby must be actively supervised at all times with this activity.** So why not join in whilst you are there and move the toys around slowly, encouraging your baby's gaze to follow whilst also talking about each item.

**What you need...**

- Rope
- Pegs or binder clips
- A variety of safe items to peg to the line

This activity can be undertaken from birth onwards. During the first few weeks and months, their vision is blurry and they can only view objects at close range. This activity provides visual stimulation and assists in spatial awareness. As their awareness increases, so too will their desire to bat at objects, assisting in hand-eye coordination.

# TACTILE TICKLES

*Gather a range of textured objects and brush them over your baby's tummy.*

**Handy Hint**
This is a great activity to do on the change table to entertain a wriggly baby whilst you are trying to change the nappy!

**What you need...**

- A range of textured objects such as feathers, and pieces of interesting material like velvet, satin, cord, etc.

Whilst this activity can be used from birth to provide tactile stimulation and body awareness for your young baby, you may find that it will last several months. In the end, it may very well become a game with your baby.

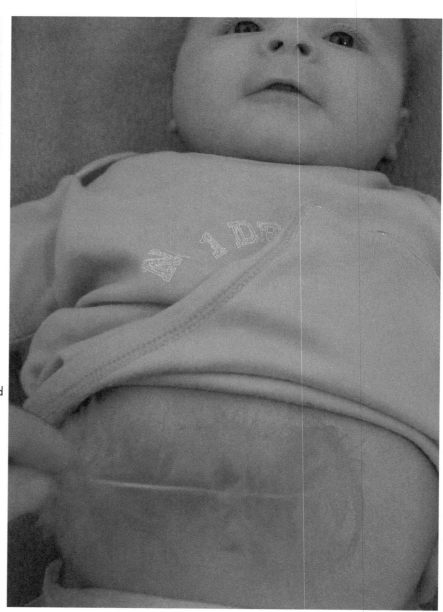

# DANCING RIBBONS

*Grab some ribbons, secure them to the end of a wooden spoon and gently wave the ribbons to entertain your baby.*

**Handy Hint**

It's really simple. There are no tricks. But my little boy just loved this one.

This activity can be undertaken from birth onwards. Initially, the movement of ribbons aids in visual-tracking skills and provides tactile stimulation. As your baby's skills progress, their hand eye coordination will be tested as they try to grab the ribbons.

**What you need...**

- Wooden spoon
- A variety of ribbons with different patterns and colours

# DANGLING NOISE

*Gather all the noisy items that you can find around the house, hang them on a ribbon and dangle them in front of your baby.*

This activity is suitable from birth onwards and assists your baby in developing their listening skills and auditory awareness. As your baby grows, they will also develop hand-eye coordination as they try to swipe at various objects.

**What you need...**

- Ribbon
- Noisy objects such as a rattle, jar lids, spoons etc.

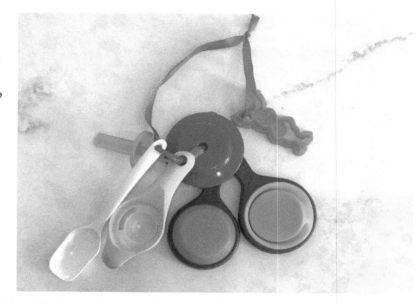

**Handy Hint**

Gently shake the objects at approximately 30cm from your baby and allow them time to locate the sound. Then try moving it to a different location and help them in following the noise.

# RAID THE CUPBOARDS

*Find some plastic measuring cups, spoons and other interesting (and safe) items from the kitchen, and place them within reach of baby on the floor allowing him to pick them up and explore them.*

Suitable from approximately 3 months and onwards, during this time your baby will be exploring the world around them. Measuring cups and other implements from the kitchen are perfect for practising dexterity and providing tactile stimulation. Both fine - and gross - motor skills get a work out with this activity.
**Be sure to maintain constant supervision and avoid small items.**

### Handy Hint

As the baby grows up and gets mobile, they are likely to still enjoy playing with objects from the kitchen for many months to come! My just-2 year old is still obsessed with unpacking the cupboards and using the kitchen objects more so than her actual toys. I find it useful to allocate a cupboard or drawer for her with safe items, such as containers, and let her access it as freely as she wants.

**What you need...**

- A random assortment of safe items from the kitchen such as plastic measuring cups

# PEEKABOO BOARD

6 - 12 months

*Got a piece of cardboard lying around, a few photos and scraps of fabric? Bam. You've got yourself a peekaboo board.*

**What you need...**

- Piece of cardboard
- Photos or pictures cut from magazines, etc.

**Handy Hint**

Stick each picture onto the board with adhesive tack. This way you can mix them up for a true surprise game of peekaboo. One day it could be family, the next farmyard animals or nature themed....

Peekaboo is a classic game that stimulates a baby's senses and helps develop their gross-motor skills and social development. At around 5 months of age, babies start learning about object permanence. This refers to the concept that even though a baby can't see something directly in front of them, they are aware that it still exists. This game is perfect for babies aged 6-12 months whilst they are relatively immobile but keen to explore the world around them.

# HIDE THE TOY

*Find a toy and put it in a box or bowl; then ask your baby 'Where is the toy?'. Watch as your baby tries to find it.*

**What you need...**

- Small toy or object
- 1–3 small boxes or bowls of varying sizes

At around 5 months old, your baby is learning about object permanence, the idea that something exists even if they cannot see it. Help guide your baby on this exploration, and use exaggerated tones when repeating phrases such as 'Is the toy in there?' whilst your baby is searching.

**Handy Hint**

This works equally well with toys hidden under a small cloth or tea towel.

# PEEKABOO SCARF

*It's really simple. Get a scarf and play peekaboo.*

**Handy Hint**

Be sure to do this slowly to help your baby process what is happening and to improve their tracking skills.

I know, I know, you think that this is too simple. But really, your little bundle of joy is just developing their understanding of the world around them. As previously mentioned, around 6 months or so, children learn about object permanence. This game helps your child understand that even when Mummy or Daddy disappear behind a scarf, they still exist. Soon you will have them giggling with joy at the game.

**What you need...**

- Scarf or cloth

# FINGER-PAINTING

6mths – 5yrs

*Allow children of all ages some sensory and creative play by grabbing some finger paint and a piece of paper (a high chair tray is fine for younger kids) and let them go nuts!*

**Handy Hint**

If you love the idea of finger-painting but hate the mess, place a few blobs of paint on a piece of paper or canvas and drape cling film (or a thicker clear plastic) on top of it. Children love running their fingers through the paint and watching it glide in all directions.

## What you need...

- Finger paint (refer to the DIY vault on page 9 for recipes)
- Paper or easy wipe surface (like high chair tray)

Whilst the thought of messy play can be scary, particularly to the obsessive parent like me, it is a crucial activity in your child's brain and muscle development. Sensory play, such as finger-painting, teaches children a broad range of skills, including motor skills, cause-and-effect skills, colour recognition, colour mixing and experimentation. Be sure to maintain a level of supervision appropriate for your child's age.

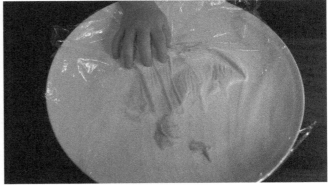

# BUBBLES BUBBLES BUBBLES

*Get bubble mix and blow the bubble mix. It's as simple as that.*

**Handy Hint**

For little children, if you blow bubbles gently towards softer materials, such as carpet or a towel, they are likely to stick longer without popping on impact and give your child a chance to 'catch' them. A bubble mix by the change table can also provide a welcome distraction for a wriggly infant!

**What you need...**

- Bubble mix (refer to our DIY vault on page 9 for a home bubble mix recipe)
- Bubble wand

The fascination with bubbles starts young. Watching bubbles float through the air helps their eye-tracking skills and hand-eye coordination. If they are lucky enough to catch it, they will begin to understand cause and effect (i.e., I caught it and it popped). Older children love chasing after them and trying to pop each and every one before they hit the ground; this is a great way to burn energy! We find that this is a wonderful activity to do on the porch on rainy days.

# MAGNET SORTING

*Got magnets on your fridge? Let the kids play with them!*

**What you need...**

- Magnets

One of the most frequented areas by children in our house is the fridge. They just love to sit there constantly whilst I am cooking. My daughter can play with the magnets for ages, sorting them and making different pictures. You can use what you have or buy some new ones. Find something with an interesting picture, and make sure that the magnet is not small and likely to fall off.

One of my daughter's favourites is an old tourist magnet that my husband has had for 10+ years from some random Australiana store with a koala on it!

Our other favourites are definitely some custom-made magnets that we created online (for very cheap, I might add) with family pictures on them. We actually bought these for my mum for her fridge, but our daughter hasn't stopped playing with them and sorting through her family members as she begins to process the people in her world.

**Handy Hint**

We recently bought a magnetic set with 4 backgrounds and about 20 different magnets that can be placed on top of these scenes. The kids love this, so I keep it hidden and bring it out when I am in the kitchen and need to keep an eye on Little Miss. In this manner, she won't tire of it before I can benefit from it!

# SPAGHETTI MADNESS

*Simply cook spaghetti until a little undercooked, wash in cold water, add a teaspoon of oil (to prevent it from sticking together), shake in a plastic bag with a very small amount of food colouring and let them create the rest!*

Sensory play allows children to explore and create through play. It is believed to be a crucial process in brain development and assisting children to undertake more complex learning tasks later on in life, including problem-solving, language development and cognitive growth. Most importantly, it's fun.

Children love exploring the texture, taste and colour of spaghetti and picking it up with their hands. I also like to add in some tongs and a few pots and pans to encourage imaginative play and help with those fine-motor skills. This is a great activity for all preschoolers to get involved in regardless of age.

Be sure to maintain constant supervision and use food appropriate for your child's age.

**What you need...**

- Cooked spaghetti
- Food colouring
- 1 tsp. oil

### Handy Hint

With older kids, suggest making a picture with the coloured spaghetti. Or try other materials for a sensory experience, such as oats, dried beans, corn kernels, rice noodles or shredded coconut. Of course, the usual safety precautions regarding younger children and choking hazards apply.

# SHAPE SORTING

*Find a box and some bottle tops or balls (or rolled-up socks),
cut some slots in the top of the box and let them learn to
pop these items in the hole. For older kids, add an element
of colour or shape sorting to the exercise.*

**Handy Hint**

Depending on the age of your child, you can colour code it and talk about the colours of each cap and which slot they should go in. Use a bigger box for walkers to get them moving. You can even tie some ribbons on there for your baby to undo.

This activity helps build cognitive and fine-motor skills and teaches object permanence. It is also a great activity that can be adapted in many ways, so children of various ages can play.

For example, for babies, it can be a simple task of placing balls or plastic caps through holes, but older children can start to differentiate shapes and colours.

Remember: If you are using plastic bottle caps, you can still make round, diamond or rectangular holes for your baby to solve how the cap needs to go into the hole (e.g., 'The round lid doesn't fit in the square hole. What if I turn it on its side?').

**What you need...**

- Cardboard box
- Plastic bottle lids (large enough so that they aren't a choking hazard) or other shaped objects

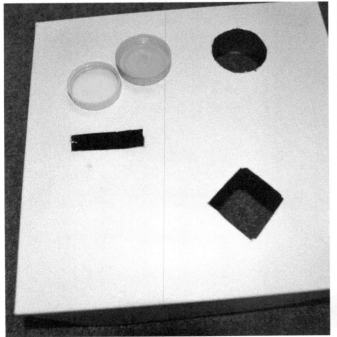

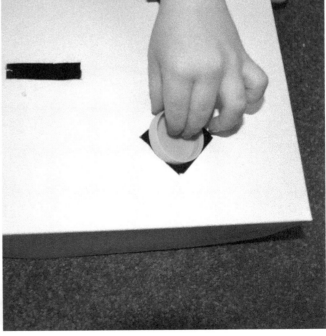

# SENSORY BALL PIT

*Grab your portable cot out and create a ball pit with the balls that you have around the house.*

**Handy Hint**
Add a bowl, a ladle and a few other items that your kids can use to scoop up the balls and extend their play.

Create your own ball pit at home, and you will ensure endless hours of fun and laughter! Sensory ball pits provide active play with sensory stimulus, relaxation, motor skills development and social interaction. By simply providing a few extra tools, like a bowl and a ladle, children enhance their exploration and learning through concepts such as cause and effect and fine-motor development.

**What you need...**

- Portable cot (a normal cot will do if the slots between the bars aren't too wide)
- Balls

# DRUMS AND OTHER INSTRUMENTS

6mths – 3yrs

*Take some kitchen bowls and a few wooden spoons, and let your baby loose.*

**Handy Hint**

Put on some music with a good beat, and let your child belt out the drums to their heart's content. As they get older, try to help them in banging to the beat. For a list of great adult songs for children, check out page 15. My son just loves playing along to Dire Straits' Sultans of Swing, and my daughter LOVES Despacito featuring Biebs and Stolen Dance by Milky Chance.

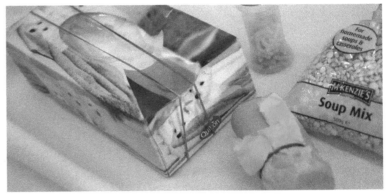

**What you need...**

- Pots and pans
- Wooden spoons

I have yet to meet a child who doesn't love a good bash on the kitchen drums. Drumming improves auditory, rhythm and cause-and-effect skills. To further improve these skills, play the following types of games with your child:

1. Copycat – Tap a simple rhythm, and then let your child repeat it back.
2. Play at different strengths, demonstrating the difference between quiet and noisy levels.
3. Sing along to the beat of The Little Drummer Boy.

You could also make a whole band with a box banjo (tissue box with elastic bands on it), maracas (empty container filled with beans), a kazoo (cardboard tube with tissue paper on one end secured with an elastic band) and rhythm blocks (some sandpaper glued to two pieces of wood). Of course, always be vigilant with young children and elastic bands and ensure constant supervision.

# WATER PLAY - BASIC

*Grab a large container of water and some play items, like a funnel, measuring cup or jugs.*

**Handy Hint**

I love to create a scene with children by adding a few of the small toy animals that we have around the house, along with rocks, sticks, leaves and other natural items.

**What you need...**

- Small container to fill with water (best with shallow sides)
- Various kitchen implements (funnels, measuring cups and spoons etc.)

One of those timeless activities that kids just love is splashing, stirring and pouring water. Water play develops motor skills, problem-solving skills, language development, social-emotional growth and even science and mathematical skills! Try introducing concepts like full, empty and half. Or test different objects —what floats, what sinks? Or add a drop of food colouring, some glitter and a little bit of dishwashing liquid, and let your child discover water whisking.
The thing that I love about water play is that it seems to have a universal calming effect, allowing kids to unwind and relax. If you have floorboards or tiles, you can simply place the container on top of some towels to help soak up splashes. Alternatively, consider relocating to an area of the bathroom, or even sitting in the bath or on the shower floor (with a non-slip mat underneath), if the idea of water in the house is too much.

**ONCE AGAIN, PLEASE REMEMBER TO ALWAYS ACTIVELY SUPERVISE ALL WATER PLAY.**

# BABY JUG EXPLORATION

6mths – 2yrs

*Simply grab a milk jug, cut off the top and cut a hole on the side, and let your baby drop the items (of a safe size) into it.*

**Handy Hint**

If you have older kids, let them take part by showing your baby how to drop things in.

This activity helps your baby in developing their fine-motor skills and learning cause and effect. They have endless enjoyment picking up the items and dropping them through the hole to hear what sounds they make and then trying to find the item again. As your baby grows, ask them to pick up a certain type of object or colour, and extend the learning further.

**What you need...**

- Large milk or juice container
- Safe items to drop into a jug. This could include plastic spoons, large bottle tops, etc.

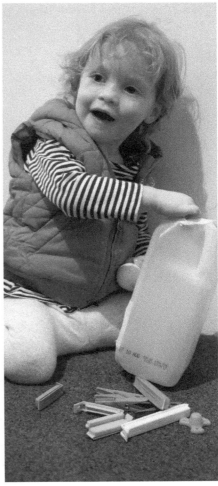

# PEEKABOO FAMILY JIGSAW

*Grab a wooden jigsaw from an op shop and cut up family photos to put in there!*

**Handy Hint**

If you already have a jigsaw at home that you don't want to ruin, simply cut the photos to size and secure them with adhesive tack so that they can be removed later.

Junior puzzles help with fine-motor skills (including pincer grip), hand-eye coordination and the concepts of size and shape. My experience with my own children has been a constant fascination with all photos of familiar people; this one is always a hit.

**What you need...**

- Wooden puzzle with removable pieces
- Photos (or pictures from a magazine)

# SHAKEN, NOT STIRRED

6mths – 2yrs

*Grab a plastic bottle, and put something in it that will make noise when you shake it (like rice, beans, etc.). After making sure it is secure by taping the lid well, give it to your baby to shake.*

**Handy Hint**

If you use a THOROUGHLY cleaned Panadol bottle, you will have the added benefit of a child safety seal to ensure that the lid is not pulled off!

A noisy toy helps encourage your baby to reach out, investigate and practise those gross-motor skills, particularly clutching an object. Once held, the satisfying noise made when shaking the bottle provides your baby with an understanding of cause and effect.

**Note: Please ensure that lid is secured tightly in a safe manner to avoid a chocking hazard and be sure to always maintain supervision.**

**What you need...**

- Clean plastic bottle with a secure lid
- Rice, beans or something else to fill the bottle with
- Packaging tape

# DISCOVERY BOX

*Grab a basket or a box, put in some items from around the home and let your baby explore.*

It doesn't matter what toys you buy, it's everyday household items that children are always drawn to! The concept behind this box is that you are allowing your baby, and even slightly older children, to explore safe household items (otherwise known as heuristic play).

The collection of items can encourage hand-eye coordination, gross-motor skills and creative play (particularly in older children), but it also enables some education on whatever theme that you choose. For younger children, this could be textures, colours or smells. For older children, you could incorporate items representative of a particular country or of a particular profession; think toothbrush (dentist), cooking utensils (chef), football, books, etc.

**Handy Hint**

I find that this works well by picking a theme: colours, fruit and vegetables, types of clothes, smells (safe herbs from the garden or even empty herb containers as they retain smell), shiny objects and whatever else you can think of.

**What you need...**

- Basket or box
- Various items of a particular theme

# MUFFIN EXPLORATION

6mths – 2yrs

*Fill the holes of a muffin tin with a variety of random safe objects such as balls of a suitable size, and allow your baby to explore it.*

**Handy Hint**

Leave some spaces so that your baby can move the objects between the slots. For older children, you can put numbers on the base of the muffin tins and have them fill them up accordingly with pom poms or other small objects. Ask them to do it with chopsticks or a spoon for even more development!

This activity promotes motor skills as well as hand-eye coordination, cause-and-effect skills and problem-solving skills. The reason I like this is that it is a particularly effective activity for that difficult age; you know, the one when they can push up and manoeuvre around and/or crawl but not yet sit or walk. This is also great for more advanced tummy time! Remember, be sure to only use balls that are large enough to not pose a choking hazard.

**What you need:**
- Muffin tray
- Balls or other objects

# VEGETABLE STAMPS

*Remember this classic from kindergarten days? Stamps don't need to be bought to be interesting. Collect the fruit and vegetables that you have around the home, cut interesting shapes in them and explore the print they make.*

This one is purely about exploration, fine-motor skills and quiet (but messy) play. You can carve shapes out of a potato or sweet potato. Or you can just let your children explore a whole variety of vegetables in their own way. You could even roll a carrot or sweetcorn across the page lengthwise or scrunch up a piece of lettuce. Lemons naturally also make a unique shape on paper, as does half an onion.

Please remember to maintain constant supervision with younger kids.

**What you need...**

- Paper
- Fruit and vegetables
- Paint

**Handy Hint**

I can hear the collective groan now with the potential mess! Remember, you don't actually need that much paint on the vegetable. Kids aren't great with wiping off the excess paint to avoid drips, so I always grab a plate and just put a little paint on the bottom for them to dip into and avoid the mess.

# TUNNEL

*Simply grab a box or two and join them together with the ends open at either side.*

**Handy Hint**
When they tire of the tunnel, poke some holes in the top and hang some socks or stockings down. Or place some balls, rattles, books, etc. in the tunnel to increase curiosity!

Once those babies are up and crawling, they are into exploring EVERYTHING! So let's give them some fun along the way. Crawling tunnels help develop motor skills and hand-eye coordination with all those exciting things to swat out of the way. Seriously, who needs a cubby?

**What you need...**
- Cardboard box(es)
- Optional: socks or stockings

# SENSORY BOTTLES

*Create a bottle full of fun, and let children explore through their senses. Find a clear, empty and clean bottle with a good lid, and fill it up with a variety of materials. These can be in suspension (i.e. water or oil) or not. Refer to pictures for inspiration.*

**Handy Hint**

For younger children, an empty spice bottle is a great size for them to observe and handle. Larger spring water bottles are great for slightly bigger kids.

Sensory bottles... where do I start?

The use of sensory bottles is prolific, and they are used for a number of reasons: to calm children down, to entertain on a long wait or car trip or to encourage mess-free sensory exploration. Sensory bottles provide a way to explore their senses whilst keeping them free from dangerous, small objects and overstimulation from tactile play.

A few of my favourite ideas for sensory bottles are shown in these pages, but a quick internet search will provide you with many, many more!

One thing to think about is the liquid that you put in the bottle and how it will affect the outcome. Some discussion on this:

- **Water** – great and easy material and helps objects to move fast, but avoid use with metallic objects or it will lead to rust.
- **Baby oil/cooking oil** – adds another visual dimension (when used with water) and allows objects to move a little slower.
- **Dishwashing detergent** – helps create bubbles and sink glitter.
- **Hair gel** – slows down the movement of objects.

**Calming Jar**

There is something enticing and calming about watching glitter settle. Watching the glitter settle helps our feisty 4 year old collect his thoughts and communicate more effectively.

*Add: a good squirt of glitter glue, warm water, a drop of food colouring and some glitter.*

As an extra bonus, add a small animal or figure aligned with your child's interests. For us, it was a superhero figurine. Then shake the bottle and watch the figurine twist and turn as the glitter slowly subsides.

**Colour-Themed Bottles (top left)**
This is a fun one to get the kids involved in filling up. Search the house for items and sort them by colours into the bottles.

**Baby Sensory Bottles (top middle)**
Baby sensory bottles can be filled with foil, pipe cleaners, buttons, pom poms and whatever else you can find!

**Magnetic Discovery Bottles (top right)**
Fill a bottle with baby oil (or mineral oil) and magnetic items, such as pipe cleaners cut into small pieces or paper clips. Give your child a magnet and let them explore!

**Book-Themed Bottles (above)**
I love love love this idea. These ones are themed for the book 'We're Going on a Bear Hunt'. So, in order we have:

- Shredded green paper (grass)
- Dyed water with oil (river)
- Mud (thick oozy mud)
- Leaves (forest)
- Cotton wool balls (snowstorm)

Get creative with your favourite book!

**Ocean-Themed Bottle (above)**
Place hair gel in a ziplock bag, and add a drop of food colouring. (It will be much darker in the bottle, so make sure that you dye it lightly.) Cut the corner of the bag, and squirt the gel into the bottle. Next, insert creatures into the bottle, and use a skewer to position them if need be.

**Other ideas include:**
Season-themed bottles
Food-related (left)
Water and Beads

# POMPOM DROP

6mths – 2yrs

*Poke a cardboard tube through the lid of a clear takeaway container, and give your child a bowl of pompoms. Let them do the rest!*

This activity is great for practising concentration, learning about cause-and-effect skills and refining those fine-motor skills.

Be sure to maintain constant supervision of your child with this activity and choose pompoms large enough to not pose a chocking hazard.

**What you need...**
- Cardboard tube
- Clear takeaway container
- Pompoms (or cotton wool balls)

**Handy Hint**

There are many ways to extend this activity. For instance, put a coloured piece of paper around each tube, and encourage your children to sort the colours. Or if you are really adventurous, you could run connections between multiple pipes and containers to create something akin to a marble run.

# FAMILY FUN

6mths – 2yrs

*Create a photo album with pictures of family and friends. Sit with your little one and name each person. You will notice that babies will continually refer back to this album.*

**Handy Hint**

Use plastic ziplock bags for the pages. Simply punch holes along the bottom edge, and bind them together with some colourful yarn. Cut pieces of cardboard to fit into each of the bags, and paste a picture on either side of the cardboard.
Now you have an easy to clean book in which to interchange pictures when needed!

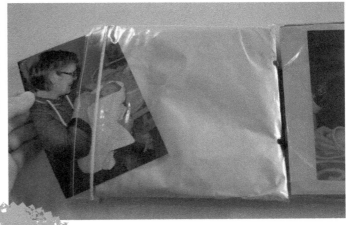

Both of my kids showed an active interest in the members of their family from an early age. We made a family photo book, and each of them would flick through it for ages and, as they grew, name each family member. Photo books help foster a sense of belonging with your child and, as we found, made it easier to leave them with family members when we needed some timeout. Other great ideas are putting a mirror in one page so that your baby can see themselves or ensuring that  the photos of each family member include your baby so that they can see how they belong, like we did with our son's photo book.

**What you need...**

- Cardboard or paper
- Photos or pictures
- Ziplock bags and yarn

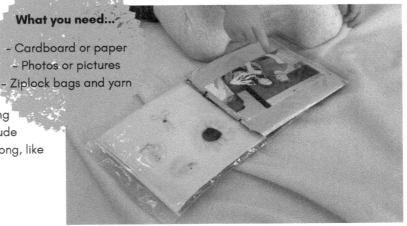

# BATHROOM FUN

*Put holes in the bottom of a container. Fill up the container at bath time, and lightly shower your baby's body.*

Anything in the bath is a hit at our house. We initially had one of these, but then one child would inevitably argue with the other over it, so we had to make another (thankfully that took all of 30 seconds). This activity shows cause and effect and helps with motor skills once they are doing it themselves. I have noticed that this is also done at the kids' swimming classes in the one to two-year-old class to help children with water familiarity and getting their head wet.  Start by doing this on an arm or leg. Then progress to the tummy or back of the head. Only shower over your baby's face when they are ready, and do it in small amounts.  As always, make sure that they are actively supervised.

**What you need...**

- Margarine (or other) plastic container

**Handy Hint**
Alternatively, create a boat out of a bottle, pool noodle, half an apple or anything else that you can find.

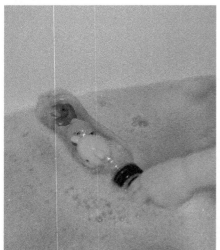

# MOUNTAIN (CUSHION) CLIMBING

6mths – 3yrs

*As your child develops their crawling and climbing skills, place cushions on the floor of different shapes and sizes, and allow your baby to climb up and down on them whilst supervised.*

Courses like this help develop gross-motor skills as well as problem-solving and cognitive skills. If you have children like mine who are natural climbers and movers, this activity will help you stay sane! Just don't expect it to come with silence...

**What you need...**

- Cushions

**Handy Hint**

This works well for older kids as well. My kids love to position animals strategically around the mountains and in the valleys. They love the challenge of 'avoiding the crocodiles', 'rescuing the owl', etc. You will quickly learn that older children like to jump on the cushions from a height (like the top of the couch), so be sure to establish the rules early!

# CUP AND SPOONS

*Spoons and cups. Spoons in cups. That's it! Strangely, my kids have always loved to sort spoons (or safe, child-appropriate forks and knives) into cups.*

Sorting items into different containers helps refine those fine-motor skills and cognitive skills. Too many spoons resting on one side? There you go, cause and effect (i.e., it topples).

Put this activity in the lifesaver bank for entertaining young toddlers in the high chair or kitchen whilst you are trying to get dinner ready.

**What you need...**

- Cups
- Spoons

**Handy Hint**

This is a great activity to whip out when you are rushing to cook dinner in the kitchen and need to keep the kids in view. Our children's plastic cutlery and cup sets are colourful, which has really added another dimension to the activity (e.g., sorting by colour) and has provided the opportunity for my eldest to get involved and teach his little sister about colours.

# SENSORY BOARD

6mths – 2yrs

*Create a board with different textured materials such as carpet, lino and bubble wrap for your child to explore*

**Handy Hint**

You can also try an activity board. Ideas include a calculator, a set of hanging keys, a few types of latches, shoes, a colander, anything!

My favourite is collecting the lids from wipes packets and sticking the material inside to add a 'peekaboo' element.

**What you need...**

- Assortment of textured fabrics, materials or floor coverings
- Large board or cardboard
- Lids from wipes

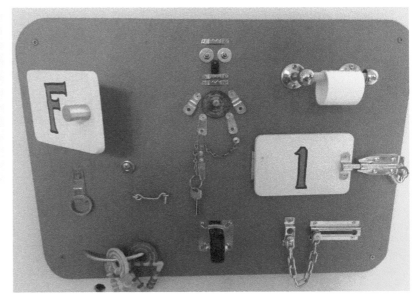

Oh, where do we start? You have fine-motor skills, cause and effect, and cognitive and problem-solving skills all in one go. And hey, it's pretty cool, right? If you really want to be advanced, you could create some peekaboo slots where the item inside is alternated as a surprise. I love, love, love this one with those crawlers who are constantly getting themselves into trouble.

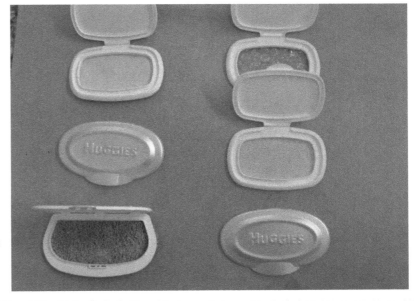

# IN THE SPOTLIGHT

*Grab a torch, secure some translucent fabric over it with an elastic band and let the coloured light dance across the room.*

**Handy Hint**
For older children's participation, teach them how to make shadow puppets on the wall. Let them explore what happens if you move your hands closer to the torch and farther away. Ask them, 'What does this do to the size of the shadow?'

Young children are fascinated by lights. Shine the light on a wall, or toy and move it slowly whilst your baby tracks where it goes. For movers, let them crawl after/follow the light before moving it elsewhere. Turn the light on and off, and ask 'Where did it go?' Or draw shapes on the wall.

This activity helps increase visual-tracking skills in younger children and hand-eye coordination and gross-motor skills in those older babies who are on the move.

**What you need...**
- Torch
- (Optional): tissue paper or translucent fabric to drape over it

# THAT'S A WRAP

6mths – 2yrs

*Have you ever noticed that younger children prefer the wrapping paper to the present? Let's cut out the middleman here, and just wrap some ordinary objects from around the house with wrapping paper.*

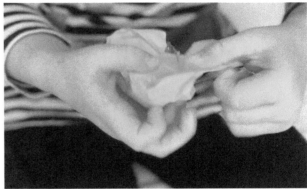

**What you need...**
- Wrapping paper of different patterns and textures
- Sticky tape
- Ordinary (and safe) objects to wrap

**Handy Hint**
Be sure to just loosely sticky tape the wrapping paper together so that bubs can get a finger under it and easily rip it open and maintain constant supervision for younger children to avoid paper in the mouth.

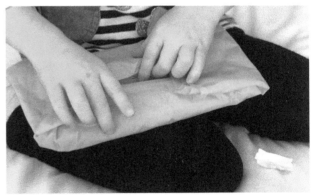

This activity helps develop your child's exploratory, problem-solving and fine-motor skills. It also helps reinforce the idea of object permanence. Whilst my daughter was more than happy to unwrap items, I included my son by adding an element of role play.

We pretended it was my birthday, wrapped a present, got an imaginary cake ready and then sang happy birthday. We were sure to open the imaginary card first (because that is the polite thing to do before opening a present), and then we opened the present. And I was careful to thank everyone for the beautiful gift.

This has helped our son and our daughter start to understand our social rituals, and (hopefully) foster an appreciative attitude when receiving presents. This is important to me because it is my ongoing fear that my child will be that child who says, 'I don't like this' or 'I already have this'.

# BABY MAZE

*Grab a towel or blanket, place a few objects on it
and help your baby navigate around them.*

**Handy Hint**
I use large objects (like a bucket or pots) for crawling babies to aid them in perceiving the obstacles and
navigating around them as opposed to barging through.

For both crawling babies and babies who are learning to walk, this maze allows them to
perceive challenges and navigate around obstacles, testing both gross-motor skills and
balance. You will be surprised at how many squeals of delight you will get whilst your
baby tries to find a safe spot for their next step.
Of course, be sure to match the level of difficulty to your child's ability and be sure to
only use safe objects to navigate around, particularly when they are unstable walkers.

**What you need...**

- Towel or blanket
- 5-6 objects spaced
  around the towel

# STACKING RINGS

*Grab a cardboard tube, plant it in play dough, cut some rings from paper plates and start stacking.*

Stacking rings is a classic game full of problem-solving and fine-motor skill development for your baby. It also helps them with size and shape discrimination.

Your baby may not be able to stack in accordance with size until 18+ months, but they will still have a ton of fun just pulling the rings off and on the pole.

**What you need...**

- Cardboard tube (e.g., a kitchen paper towel roll)
- Paper plates or other rings

**Handy Hint**

If you feel the urge, you can colour the rings and make them different sizes to help your baby learn colours (i.e., put the green one on next).

# JUNIOR SCAVENGER HUNTS

*Create a scavenger hunt sheet, and get your kids to hunt the items around the house. It doesn't need to be complicated, just draw a few items, such as blocks, a hairbrush, a ball, a doll, a shoe, a spoon, etc., and hide them around the room or house.*

**Handy Hint**

There are so many variations of this that you can do. Here are just a few:

- ABC Hunt - get kids to go around the house and grab an item starting with each letter of the alphabet
- Colour Hunt - grab a few paint chips from the local hardware store and get your children to bring back items that closely match those colours
- Puzzle hunt - get your children to find all the pieces of a puzzle that are hidden around the house and complete the puzzle along the way

Scavenger hunts get kids moving! It enhances gross-motor skills, visual-perceptual skills, and cognitive skills. The best thing is you are guaranteed to have a little quiet time (hopefully enough time to make some coffee) whilst they are off searching the house!

**What you need...**

- Various items to hide around the house

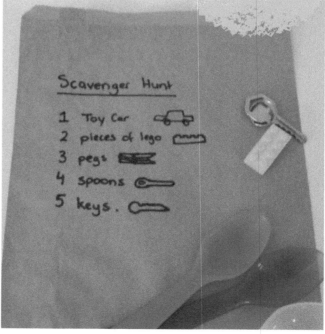

# OBSTACLE COURSE

*Grab a number of items around the house and get creative with an obstacle course. Be sure to add in items that will include a variety of actions, such as jumping, crawling, etc.*

**Handy Hint**

This is a great one to burn off that endless toddler energy. Try timing it (or in my case, pretending to at least), and you'll have a child who wants to do it over and over again to try and improve their time! A wonderful way to create one very exhausted kid.

**What you need...**

- Hula hoops, tape, cushions, chairs, beanbags, tables, Tupperware or whatever else you can find

This activity is a favourite with my kids, and it usually extends from our lounge room to the kitchen and hallway.

Some activities ideas include:

- Using a chair to crawl under
- Cushions to climb over
- A line of tape to use as a tightrope with dangerous animals on either side (usually our toy crocodile, dinosaur or owl)
- A hoop to jump through

# BALL TOSS

*Simply find a ball, soft toy or rolled-up pair of socks and a laundry basket, then start throwing.*

**Handy Hint**
If you want to create some hacky sacks or balls at home, why not try the ones listed on page 12.

There are plenty of variations here depending on your child's skill level and the materials you have available. Here are just a few to get you thinking:
- Place a few baskets on the floor, and put points on them depending on distance.
- Hang a basket over a door handle or on stairs to add some height.
- Create a ramp with a cardboard box in front of the baskets, and roll the ball up the ramp and into the basket.
- Tape lines on the floor for children to progressively move back as they improve.

**What you need...**
- Balls, hacky sacks, rolled socks or soft toys
- Laundry basket or other box

# BOWLING

*Set out plastic cups as the pins, grab a ball and start a bowling alley in the hallway.*

**Handy Hint**

For younger children, stack the cups into a pyramid formation to increase the strike rate.

What is it with kids and knocking things down? This game is great for kids learning to take turns and co-operate, problem-solving skills and gross-motor skills.

**What you need...**

- Plastic cups or empty drink bottles
- Balls

# SOCCER

*Set up soccer goals with anything you can find
(chairs or cups work well) and have a kickoff (with a
soft ball of course)*

**Handy Hint**
If you have a few hours to fill, you could extend this activity by
creating the Olympics. You could combine this activity with
bowling, sumo wrestling and several other activities in this book.

Soccer is a great sport to help with balance,
coordination, hand-eye skills and working as a team.
If you have the next budding soccer superstar, you could
also try combining this with Red Light, Green Light to test
their stopping skills.

**What you need...**

- Cones or chairs
- Soft ball

# SNOWBALL FIGHT

*Create a snowball fight with a whole bunch of crumpled paper. It's very simple, but it works. Let the kids run around the house, and duck and weave for cover.*

This activity helps develop gross-motor skills, hand-eye coordination and problem-solving skills. A great way to extend this game is to mark two lines on the ground with masking tape approximately 1.5m apart.
Each child takes a side and has an equal amount of snowballs. When the timer starts, they have to throw the snowball to the other player's side. When the timer goes off, the player with the least amount of snowballs wins.

**Handy Hint**
Towards the end of the activity, you can grab a basket and create a game by asking, 'Who can throw the most snowballs into the basket?'
That's it. Clean-up done!

**What you need...**

- Paper

# DANCE PARTY

*Find some high intensity music and get boogying.*

**Handy Hint**

It's always great to have a dark room and disco lights. But if you don't have that, why not give the kids torches with cellophane over the light to wave around.

**What you need...**

- Awesome music

This activity is REALLY self-explanatory, but why not incorporate it into your weekly routine. We typically play music from 4.30pm to get the kids moving before dinner (otherwise they sit around waiting for it).

Friends of ours do weekly music appreciation nights to expose their children to a wide range of music. You never know, you may have a child who ends up sharing your taste in music!

If you want some ideas for child-friendly adult songs, then check out Chapter 4 (page 15).

# TEDDY BEAR'S PICNIC

**1 – 5 years**

*Grab a picnic rug and a crew full of teddy bears and enjoy a picnic with the gang.*

**What you need...**
- Food
- Picnic rug
- Teddy bears

**Handy Hint**

If you have a gingerbread man cookie cutter, you can use it to cut your children's sandwiches, cheese or biscuits into appropriately themed shapes.

My kids love playing the 'Teddy Bears Picnic' song whilst we have our picnic. And if they are really good, they may just get a teddy bear biscuit too.

My grandfather always told me to eat the feet first to make sure that they wouldn't run away!

REAL KIDS, REAL PLAY | 69

# CLAY PLAY

*Make some clay, and let your child loose to create wonderful animals and creatures.*

**Handy Hint**

A packet of toothpicks is invaluable for clay play to connect heads, legs and arms well. Also, the garlic press makes wonderful hair!

**What you need...**

- Clay (checkout Chapter 3 for a homemade clay recipe)

Like play dough, clay is a great material for children to explore and get creative with. Whilst younger children are happy just playing with their hands, feeling the texture and refining their fine-motor skills in making basic shapes, try introducing rolling pins, shaping knives (blunt, of course) and other tools for older toddlers to create detailed creatures.

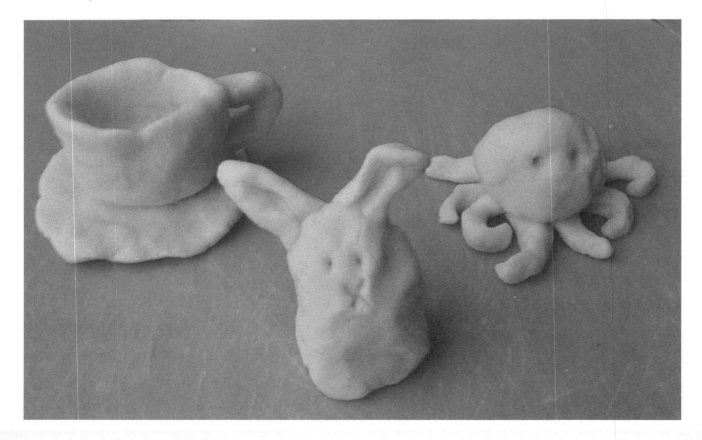

# FLYING SAUCERS

*Get some cardboard or paper plates, and create frisbees, flying saucers or boomerangs for your children to experiment with.*

**Handy Hint**
Try experimenting with the different shapes depicted below to see which ones go farther.

Frisbees and boomerangs help increase problem-solving skills, gross and fine-motor skills and hand-eye coordination. Whilst usually an outdoor activity, those made simply out of cardboard or paper plates can be used indoors for safer play.

**What you need...**

- Cardboard or paper plate

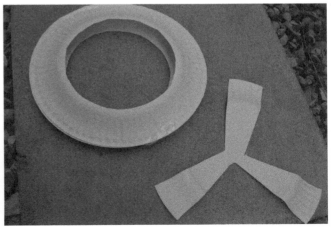

# PASTA JEWELLERY

1 – 5 years

*You remember this activity from your preschool days, right? Simply thread coloured pasta onto some string to create jewellery that your mother had to pretend she loved!*

**Handy Hint**

If you tape the end of the ribbon or string to a matchstick, it will make it much easier for little fingers to thread through pasta. It is also handy to tape the other end to the table so the pasta doesn't thread right off.

I think everyone made these in our younger days. Not only does it encourage creativity, but this activity is also great for concentration, problem-solving and fine-motor skills. Instructions are:

1. Place uncooked pasta in a plastic container or ziplock bag, and add a drop of either hand sanitiser or vinegar (this will help distribute colour).

2. Add a drop of colour, close the container (or ziplock bag) and shake to distribute colour.

3. Empty onto some baking paper, and allow it to dry.

4. Thread pasta onto string or ribbon, and create your own masterpiece.

**Note: Dried pasta can be a chocking hazard. Please maintain constant supervision.**

### What you need...

- Tube pasta
- Ziplock bags or a container
- Hand sanitiser or vinegar
- Food colouring
- String or ribbon

# PIN THE TAIL...

*Peg a tea towel to the bottom of each child's T-shirt, and let them chase each other in fits of laughter trying to steal each other's tail.*

Our friend introduced us to this one when we were trying to get two minutes of peace for the adults to eat a civilised dinner. It quickly became a family favourite!
There's not much of a trick to it; we just let the kids run wild and try to steal each other's tail. If your tail is gone, you are out.
But it's not like toddlers adhere to those rules anyway!

**What you need...**

- Pegs
- Tea towels

**Handy Hint**
When the kids are sick of chasing each others tail, we extended the game by clipping the teatowels to each shoulder and playing superheroes. We hid a doll under pillows and the kids had to 'rescue' them!

# ANIMAL WASHING STATION

*Grab a tub of soapy water and some scrubbing brushes or old toothbrushes, and start washing those animals.*

**What you need...**
- Tub
- Scrubbing brush
- Toy animals or dinosaurs
- Mud (optional)

**Handy Hint**
Add in a tub of mud to make those animals truly dirty prior to being washed.

The simplest activities are always the best! My son loved setting up a dinosaur washing station and spent ages making them REALLY dirty and then scrubbing and drying them. This activity can be expanded upon by incorporating the washing station into a wider scene. It doesn't need much—a simple green piece of fabric, and you have an outdoor scene. Chuck a cushion under the cloth, and you have mountains!

Note: Please maintain constant supervision of children around water.

# MILK PLASTIC

**Handy Hint**

Use cookie cutters to cut shapes and paint it when dry to make Christmas tree decorations (remember to add a hole before they dry!)

**What you need...**

- 1 cup milk
- 4 tbsp. white vinegar

*Combine milk and vinegar together, squeeze out liquid, shape and let dry!*

I couldn't believe it when I heard that you could make plastic out of vinegar and milk, but it's true!

Simply warm the milk in the microwave until warm but not boiling (approximately 1 minute), add 4 tbsp. of white vinegar and stir for approximately 1 minute (until curdled). Then drain the mixture and pat out excess moisture in paper towel.

You can then mould the mixture into any shape you like and leave on the paper towel to dry (approximately 2 days).

Chemically, I am led to believe that this is not exactly the same as plastic, but to the untrained eye, who would know?

# CONSTRUCTION SITE ANTICS

1 – 5 years

*Rocks and trucks, need we say more?*

**Handy Hint**

If you don't have a supply of little rocks on hand, your child is still mouthing items or you simply don't want them in the house, give cereal a try.

My son could play with rocks and trucks for hours. In fact, given his love of playing in the dirty rocks at the front of our house, I bought him a sandpit. But he just kept playing in those rocks.

On an indoor day, you can bring something similar indoors via a large storage crate. Other elements that you could add are a (cardboard) ramp or a small pond (in a cup).

Note: please fully supervise younger children to ensure that they do not place small rocks in their mouths.

**What you need...**

- A variety of small trucks and cars
- Small rocks (or cereal)

# BATHROOM PAINTING

*Paint on tiles whilst in the bath.*

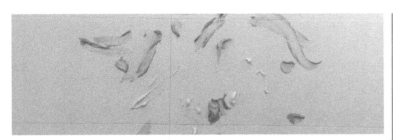

### Handy Hint

You can put the different paint colours in an ice cube tray and leave a few empty spots so that they have room to mix new colours.

If you're like me, you know the importance of messy play but groan at the thought of actually having to conduct it in your own house and clean up afterwards.

This activity has been an absolute hit for our kids and is in the best place for it; it easily washes off the walls. Furthermore, painting is an activity that helps develop your child's creativity and expression, appreciation for colours, knowledge of shapes and textures, fine-motor skills, concentration and hand-eye coordination.

**What you need...**

- Bath paint (refer to page 10)

# STAINED GLASS WINDOWS

*Stick some clear contact onto the window with the sticky side out, and let the kids decorate it with coloured paper or other craft materials.*

**Handy Hint**
Try a few variations, such as drawing a sheep on the contact with a permanent marker and letting your child make a woolly sheep with cotton wool balls or playing Pin the Tail on the Donkey/Dinosaur/ Animal.

Arts and crafts encourage fine-motor skills, control, patience, flexibility, bonding and having fun! The benefit of an unfamiliar activity such as this is that it can also act as a self-esteem booster for your children when they accomplish it!

**What you need...**

- Clear contact film
- Sticky tape to secure contact to window
- A variety of craft materials

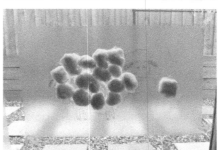

# CAR RAMPS

1 – 5 years

*So simple but such a winner. Place a large piece of cardboard (or other materials, like a plastic tray, etc.) at an angle, and roll down items such as cars.*

**What you need...**

- Piece of cardboard
- Cars and other items to roll down the ramp

**Handy Hint**

Why not combine this with the car garage (on page 138) for the full car experience?!

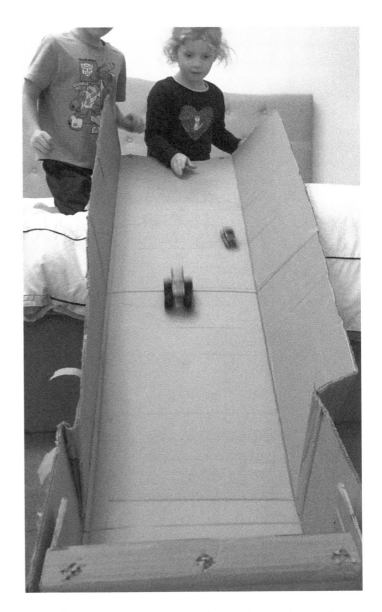

We love setting this game up at the bottom of our staircase, and it keeps the kids going for ages. To extend the play, we tend to do the following:

- Play games such as whose car can go the furthest after the ramp.
- Experiment with other items to see how fast they go down the ramp. Do round items go faster than other shapes (such as dolls, blocks etc.)?
- What happens if we put the ramp on a steeper slope? A shallower slope? A longer ramp?

Playing with cars and ramps helps your children start to understand simple physics concepts, such as motion, force and gravity.

With older preschoolers, try experimenting with cars of different sizes. Which travel faster, heavier or lighter? And what happens with more of a push (more force) or less of a push (less force)?

# BUILDING BLOCKS

*Sick of regular blocks? You can build on a grand scale with that bulk lot of toilet paper sitting in the cupboard.*

We have only one rule for this game: no opening the rolls. It's amazing how long this activity keeps my kids engaged. Each child plays with the items in slightly different ways and makes different arrangements. Beyond the quietness that this activity affords, it also helps them practise their engineering skills, gross and fine-motor skills and cause and effect all at the same time. We have also made building blocks from timber pieces at home. Be sure to sand down the rough edges when you cut a length of timber; then paint them and away you go. A hint when using timber pieces is to make sure you provide some uniformity in the shapes that you cut so that they are easier to build with.

**What you need...**

- Toilet paper rolls

**Handy Hint**

Think about what other building supplies you could use. Disposable cups and a few sticks can help build a tower for the slightly older children. Or collect some 1L milk cartons, cut the top off, stuff with newspaper and fold over the lid to make a lightweight and wipeable block!

# POMPOM PLAY

1 – 5 years

*Just tape a cardboard tube(s) to a wall and have your children drop pom poms down them into a bowl.*

For younger children, they love to watch the ball drop through a tube and pop out the other end.

As they grow, create an increasingly exciting course with channels progressively running down the wall into a container on the floor. If you have a variety of different balls, experiment with all of them; which ones go faster, the heavier, lighter, bigger, smaller or smoother ones?

Note: Pompoms can pose a choking hazard. Please maintain constant supervision of younger children.

**What you need...**

- Cardboard tubes
- Pompoms or appropriately sized balls

**Handy Hint**

You can also make this into an additional game for older children, such as a colour sorting game or a really complex ball run with both open and closed channels (refer to photos).

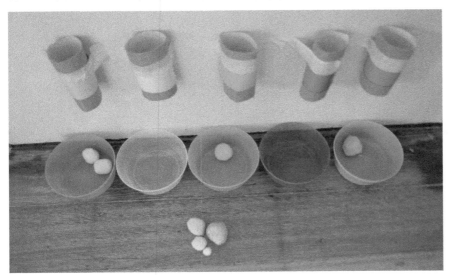

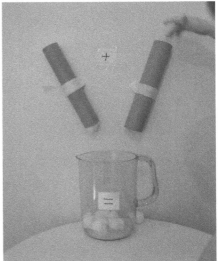

# COLOURING ON WINDOWS

**1 – 5 years**

*Need a bit of variety in your painting activities? Give painting on a vertical surface with window paints a try (refer to page 11 for DIY recipe).*

**Handy Hint**

If you have whiteboard markers, you can start by drawing a mosaic and then encouraging your children to do some colouring.

**What you need...**

- Window paints (refer to page 11)

This activity encourages fine-motor skills, control, patience, flexibility, bonding and having fun! The benefit of an unfamiliar activity such as this is that it can also act as a self-esteem booster for your children when they accomplish it.

My kids absolutely LOVE this activity. On a dreary day, just playing at the window seems to connect them to their favourite place: the outside world.

# TREASURE CHEST

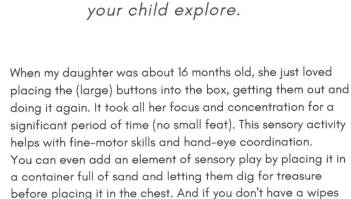

*Grab an empty wipes container and a few treasures, and let your child explore.*

When my daughter was about 16 months old, she just loved placing the (large) buttons into the box, getting them out and doing it again. It took all her focus and concentration for a significant period of time (no small feat). This sensory activity helps with fine-motor skills and hand-eye coordination.

You can even add an element of sensory play by placing it in a container full of sand and letting them dig for treasure before placing it in the chest. And if you don't have a wipes container, a tissue box makes a perfect substitute.

**Handy Hint**

For older children, hide the treasure chest around the house, make a pirate hat and map and find it.

My son also loves to cover the box with a towel, get two chopsticks and cross them over to create the 'X marks the spot'.

**What you need...**

- Empty wipes container (or tissue box)
- A variety of appropriately sized treasures, such as buttons, bottle caps, etc.
- Sand in a box (optional)

# MATCHING GAME

*This is a deck of cards matching game. You can match by colour, design or number.*

**Handy Hint**

Try to select a deck of cards with simple pictures and designs to help your child focus.

There are many ways that this game can operate. Make it simple for younger children by finding red cards, diamonds or the ones with kings. For older children, you can ask them to try and order the numbers. Or you could set out the numbers with one missing and see if they can pick up which number it is.

And then there is the memory game. Of course, limit it to perhaps 3 pairs to start with. Let your child pick out 2 cards, and see if they are a pair (a pair being the same number or the same suit). If not, turn them back over and try again.

**What you need...**

- Deck of cards

# SNOW PAINTING

*If snow is the reason that you are stuck inside, colour some water, grab some paintbrushes and start painting that ice!*

**Handy Hint**

If snow is not the reason you are playing indoors but you would still like to try this with your kids, use shredded coconut or shaved ice (if available).

**What you need...**

- Water
- Food colouring
- Snow (or coconut)

This is a messy play activity that isn't so messy. It's fun and a little different. Best of all, it's safe for younger children too.

This activity increases fine-motor skills and allows for the experimentation of colour mixing and the added lesson of learning about ice melting!

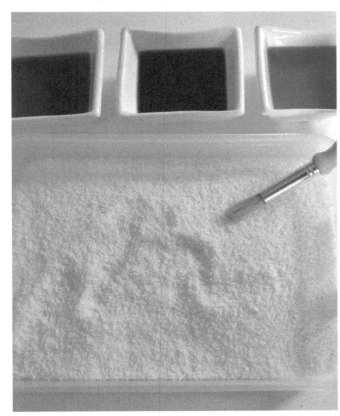
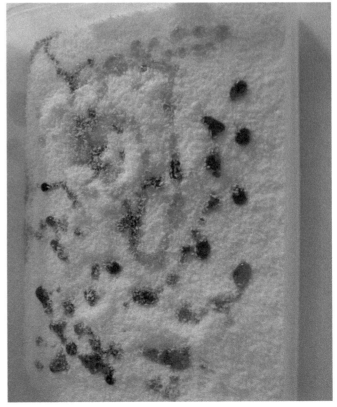

# PAPER AEROPLANES

*Make a paper aeroplane, create a target with a sheet of paper on the door frame or a laundry basket and start flying!*

This is another one of those activities that can be adjusted in many ways depending on the child's age. For younger children, you really don't need a target, just the art of flying the plane alone will be enough. As their paper prowess increases, add in a landing strip. That is, some tape on the floor by which you can mark how far each plane went (cue here the competition). You can then add a large target like a washing basket on the floor or, if super confident, a hanging target from the door frame with different holes. And be sure to add an element of experimentation with older kids. Try various designs and folds to see which plane works the best.

**Handy Hint**

Our family has researched the art of paper aeroplanes an AWFUL lot. Try making a plane from a straw with two rings of paper (one smaller at the front and one larger at the back).
OK, so it's technically not all paper, but it works extraordinarily well, right?

**What you need...**

- Paper (optional)
- Targets, tape for landing strip

# INDOOR CAMPING

1 – 5 years

*Create a camping scene in your lounge room with a small tent (or sheet draped over two chairs) and sleeping bags.*

Whilst I love the idea of taking the kids camping, right now I cannot even contemplate the thought of what ACTUAL camping with 2 kids under 4 years old would bring!

That said, it appears that every child I know is obsessed with the idea of camping. It's the combination of tents, sleeping bags and campfires that really gets them excited.

If you can, add a river (piece of blue cloth) and fishing (refer to page 129). You could even 'toast' marshmallows (or pieces of banana) over the campfire.

**What you need...**

- Tent (or sheet hung over two chairs)
- Sleeping bag or blanket

**Handy Hint**

It is great to add in a few extra elements to this. Got a piece of red or orange fabric? Great, use that as a campfire. You could even grab a pot to put on top! Have a piece of blue fabric? Great, that'll serve as a little lake in which to go fishing.

# SPONGE TOWER

*This is quite simple. All you need is some colourful sponges cut into fingers, and you can let your child try and build their tower.*

This activity is great for enhancing those fine-motor skills and problem-solving abilities. You will likely find that it takes them a number of attempts to understand that the tower needs to be built on a good foundation and that stacking should be undertaken in a well-organised grid.

I found that if we got a piece of sticky tape and taped it onto the wall for the height of the tower that we achieved, this gave my eldest a great benchmark to try and beat (it's all about winning at his age!). And when you're finished, you can turn these fingers into sponge balls (refer to page 143).

**Handy Hint**

Remember Jenga? For older kids, set up the tower and try to remove one sponge finger at a time. You could even allocate a colour to each child to add to the degree of difficulty.

It's a hard one, as the sponges are rough, but my kids get sheer delight when the tower falls down!

**What you need...**

- Clean sponges

# HIDE AND SEEK

*Umm, I think you know the game...*

### Handy Hint

Have you ever tried playing Hide and Seek with a younger child who doesn't understand the concept? They run and hide (in the same place), and then they come out and show you where they were. I played this a lot with my 22-month-old when she was hanging from my leg as I was trying to get dinner done.

### What you need...

- A lot of patience!

You won't believe it, but even simple games like Hide and Seek have great benefits. Essentially, it is the next step up from Peekaboo, which has cognitive benefits and teaches children about object permanence. Whilst hiding, your children are problem-solving and trying to find the best solution (i.e., the best hiding spot) or trying to find their friends. They are also enhancing their social skills (i.e., taking turns, dealing with conflict and trial and error) whilst also getting that important physical activity. This includes improving balance, coordination and agility.

Please remember with hide and seek to point out any no-go areas or ground rules before you start (i.e., don't go out the front door, don't go upstairs, etc.). And another great hint is to have a signal in case you can't find your children or you need them to come out at any time. For us, it is a particular song.

And the best thing about this game? The more clutter you have around the house, the more places there are to hide under or around. See, you're doing them a favour!

# AIR BALL

*Set up a fan, get some lightweight balls or balloons and watch the havoc unfold!*

**Handy Hint**

Do you have ducted heating like us? Place a balloon on the grate, and it will dance around in the air whilst the heating is on! Let the kids bounce around trying to catch it.

**What you need...**

- A safe fan (please ensure that little fingers cannot get in there!)
- Balloon (or other lightweight ball)

I love this game. It is so simple but really was a heap of amusement for both my kids, particularly the youngest.

It enhances hand-eye coordination when catching the balloon and throwing it towards the fan. It also enhances a child's understanding of cause and effect and problem-solving.

This is an activity that requires constant supervision, but it is a bundle of fun and burns off a whole heap of energy!

Please be sure to be mindful of trip hazards and the safety of your child's little fingers.

# I SPY BOTTLE

*Fill a bottle with rice and a number of various small objects, and let your child try and find everything inside. For older kids, you can add a chart for them to mark off everything that they see.*

**Handy Hint**

This is a great addition to any road trip or occasion where you have a lot of sitting time (i.e., doctor appointments, plane trips and trips to Nana in the hospital).

**What you need...**

- A secure bottle
- Rice
- Various small objects for bottle

OK, so this is really a variation on the sensory bottles. But I thought that it deserved its own space because it has a great function.

Allow your child to roll the bottle over and over, and a new item will appear every time. A chart can really help extend this activity by encouraging them to mark off every item.

Finding all the items will help them develop their language skills and problem-solving skills. But above all else, it helps keep the peace and encourage some quiet time.

**Note: Please ensure bottle is securely sealed to avoid choking hazards.**

# PASTA STACK

*Place straws into play dough, and let your child try to place tubes of pasta onto the straws.*

**Handy Hint**

This activity is great for my youngest in the high chair whilst I am trying to get dinner ready. I can help her as needed, but otherwise she is more than happy to practise over and over as I am cooking and watching her.

This activity is great to expand those fine-motor skills, concentration and problem-solving abilities. I used the biggest tube pasta that I could find for my 2 year old. Then my son joined in, so I found some smaller tubes for him to add to the degree of difficulty.

**Note: Dried pasta can pose a choking hazard. Be sure to maintain constant supervision.**

**What you need...**

- Straws
- Play dough
- Tube pasta

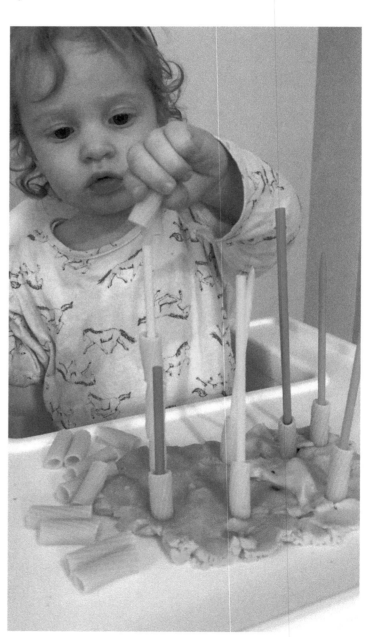

# COLOUR WHEEL

*This is pretty self-explanatory. Create a wheel out of cardboard, and then divide it into segments based on colour. Colour each peg, and let them match them up.*

**Handy Hint**

This is another great game to have on hand when you anticipate another waiting room at the doctor or dentist's office.

**What you need...**

- Cardboard
- Pegs
- Pictures, paint or textas

I admit, this may take a little over 5 minutes to construct. But it will be well worth it for a plane trip or waiting room. For older children, you can also make a counting or an alphabet wheel.

As with everything, once they have mastered it, squeeze a little more life out of it by creating a race (i.e., 'Let's time you to see how fast you can do it/whether you can beat your previous time', etc.).

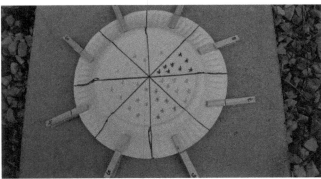

# MIRROR, MIRROR ON THE WALL

1 – 3 years

*Make faces together whilst looking into a mirror.*

**Handy Hint**

I keep some masks or hand puppets behind me so that when the activity is slowing down, I can bring them out to surprise her (in a giggly good way).

**What you need...**

- Mirror

OK, I know that this one sounds too simple. But have you ever watched a younger child with a mirror? This is a key developmental activity for self-exploration as well as learning about cause and effect, and it is even better if you play too.

Make some faces in the mirror, and see if your child can copy you. Demonstrate various expressions, such as happy, sad or angry, and let them try to copy you.

Then be silly. Act like a monkey, do jumps, wiggle or stretch yourself tall (if you have a full-length mirror). You can actually work up a sweat with this one more than you think, or maybe it's just my post-baby fitness...

Be sure to switch roles back and forth so your child learns about taking turns, leading and imitating.

# POST OFFICE

*Get a cardboard box, cut a posting slit in the top
and cut a door in the bottom to retrieve all the mail
that your child will put in there.*

**Handy Hint**

Find a small bag for your child and some envelopes, and let them collect, post
and then deliver the mail to their friends (i.e., teddies), just like the postman
does.

**What you need...**

- Cardboard box

No joke, this was my son's favourite toy for a good 3 months as a 2 year old. So much for
every expensive toy we ever owned; a cardboard box with a slit was all we needed.
Every single day we were chasing up bills and documents that had been posted away. This was really the start
of his imaginative play era. It increases fine-motor skills (or dexterity) and fosters an understanding of social
interactions.

# BALLOON GAMES - BASIC

*Kids and balloons. They don't require much explanation.*

Balloons are an age-old toy that kids just seem to love. They help enhance gross-motor skills and visual-tracking skills. For younger kids, it is simply a matter of batting the balloon over the head and trying to keep it off the ground or batting it to each other.

You can always extend the play further with a few simple rules as their skills grow:

1. Don't let the balloon touch the ground.
2. Juggle the balloon, or see if you can catch it backwards.
3. Hit back and forward, and see how many times you can do it before it drops.
4. Create an 'air target' like an open cupboard, or door, and see if you can hit it through from a distance.
5. Play balloon hockey with an open box or laundry basket serving as the goal.

**What you need...**

- Balloons!

**REMEMBER: BURST BALLOONS CAN BE A SERIOUS CHOKING HAZARD. FOR YOUNG KIDS, THEY MUST BE SUPERVISED IN THESE ACTIVITIES AT ALL TIMES.**

### Handy Hint

Try hanging the balloon in a doorway at a height that your child can just reach by jumping and see how many times they can jump and tap it. Strangely they love it and it is a great way to tire them easily!

Do you remember those balloon covers that came out in the 80's? Well, they are still available! We have one at home and it helps keep our youngest safe from burst balloons. It actually turns the balloon into more of a ball and provides the weight to kick it around whilst being totally storable at the end of the day. A great (and small) investment.

"

# NO ONE CAN BE SAD WHEN THEY HAVE A BALLOON!

WINNIE THE POOH

# TODDLER BALANCE BEAM

*Get a piece of wood on the floor, and try to tightrope across it.*

**Handy Hint**
For younger children, a piece of masking tape along the floor will be all that they need.

This helps to increase balance, coordination and concentration. It is also a hit with those budding gymnasts. I was at a store recently that sold toddler balance beams for $80! Ridiculous, I know, when a piece of timber will do just fine.

Your child will undoubtedly require handholding initially as they try to balance across the beam. But as they get bigger and older, you can spice it up by asking them to walk backwards, sideways, like a spider or with high knees across it.

Be sure to find a small piece of wood for your child, and place it on a blanket or carpet to provide your child with soft surrounds and protect any floorboards!

**What you need...**

- Long piece of timber

# ACTIVITY JAR

*Have a jar full of activities written down, and grab one at a time for your child to get all their sillies out!*

Some indoor days, it is just impossible to get all that energy out, and I know with my son that if I don't engage him quickly he will destroy our house, one brick at a time. With a simple list of wiggly activities placed in a jar, you can try and get out as much energy as possible.

Some ideas include:

- Hop to the bedroom and back.
- Spider crawl across the room.
- Run around a mat 10 times, being sure not to step on it or risk having to start again.
- Pretend you are playing air guitar for Old MacDonald.
- Make up your own silly dance for the duration of a minute.

**What you need...**

- Jar or bowl
- List of wiggly activities

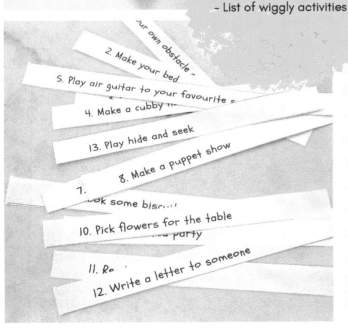

**Handy Hint**

Our house is laid out in a manner that if we open 4 doors, there is effectively a wall that our son can just run around and around and around.

One day (OK, it wasn't turning out to be a great day), I told him to run around it 30 times whilst I counted. And you know what, he did. Then he asked me to count whilst he did it again!

It has actually become a regular staple when I need some indoor energy burnt off. A few comments like, 'Oh, I think you were faster that time', or, 'Pretend a crocodile is following you', and he is in heaven. Seriously.

# ICE CUBE SORT

*Grab a bunch of cotton wool balls, pompoms (or other appropriate items), and let your child sort them into an ice cube tray.*

This activity is a winner for fine-motor skills, coordination and problem-solving. I find that it is even better (though not essential) if you have coloured pompoms so that your children can choose to sort them by colour into coloured bowls.

**What you need...**

- Ice cube tray
- A variety of small items such as cotton wool balls. Be sure to select items appropriate to your child's age.

**Handy Hint**
I always like to find an activity that both my children can engage in and which extends their skills (it makes my life easier). For my eldest, I increased the level of difficulty by giving him a pair of tweezers to move the cotton wool balls into the tray with.

# GROSS MOTOR SKILLS

*Fill a tub with water and some objects. Grab a ladle and ask your child to ladle the objects from the full tub to an empty bowl.*

**Handy Hint**

For older kids, let them try and experiment by picking up with tongs instead.

This activity is great for improving both gross and fine-motor skills, hand-eye coordination and concentration. Make sure to do this on tiles or boards, rather than carpet, and put a towel under your child and the containers. Getting wet is almost unavoidable with the littlies.
As with all water-based play, be sure to provide constant supervision.

**What you need...**

- Small tub of water
- Empty bowl
- Ladle
- A variety of safe appropriately sized items. E.g. ping-pong balls, plastic animals, etc. Try to choose some items that sink and others that float.

# STOCKING FUN

*Cut a leg from an old pair of pantyhose, stuff it with newspaper and tie it around your child's waist.*

## What you need...

- Pair of old stockings
- Something for stuffing such as newspaper or old pillow stuffing

I had totally forgotten about this activity from my childhood, and it is so simple. If your child is anything like mine, he is OBSESSED with dinosaurs.

But there are other things that you can do with pantyhose. For example, stuff the lower end with stuffing, and then tie it off to create a little doll. Bring out some markers, and put a face on it, and if you are feeling really enthusiastic, grab some yarn and sew/stick it on the top for some hair.

I have actually created a happy, sad, angry and excited doll to discuss emotions with my children. For example, you could be reading a book and ask, 'What do you think Lucy is feeling right now in the book? Can you show me which doll is sad like Lucy?'

## Handy Hint

If the thought of painting indoors doesn't scare you off completely, give painting the tail like a dalmatian, tiger or cat a try. This is best suited for thicker stockings.

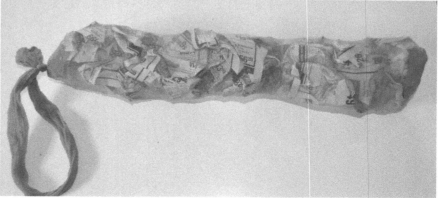

# SOCK MATCHING

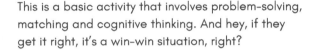

1 – 3 years

*Find 3-4 pairs of socks, and line up one of each pair in a row. Give your child the remaining socks, and ask them to match them by putting the matching sock on top of the other one.*

**Handy Hint**

I find this to be a superb activity to keep them occupied and included whilst I am folding the washing.

This is a basic activity that involves problem-solving, matching and cognitive thinking. And hey, if they get it right, it's a win-win situation, right?

For younger kids, I limit it to 3-4 pairs and make sure that they are very different from each other in terms of print and colour.

For older kids, I jumble up the socks really well and add a number of pairs that are very similar but slightly different from each other. This requires my son's full concentration to get it right.

**What you need...**

-A variety of sock pairs (Be sure to find different colours and patterns.)

# STICKY BALL CHALLENGE

1 – 3 years

*Simply wrap a ball with the sticky side of the masking tape on the OUTSIDE of the ball, and let your children figure out the rest.*

**What you need...**

- Ball
- Masking tape

**Handy Hint**

With younger children, you can watch them figure out how the ball sticks to them, and then guide them to test to what other surfaces or objects the ball sticks.

I am sure that this activity helps in their problem-solving and fine-motor skills. But most of all, it just keeps them entertained.

There are simple variations that you can make to this, like filling a tray with glitter, coconut or something else and letting them cover the ball with it. Beware: This will get messy!

# CRUNCHY CONSTRUCTION

**1 – 3 years**

*What kid doesn't like to crush and destroy things? Use a toy hammer or soft meat tenderiser, potato masher or egg flip and some crunchy cereal, and let them crush everything.*

**Handy Hint**

The more destruction that kids can reap, the better. So you could always try stacking the cereal in a big mound before you start so that their demolition has a bigger effect!

Over and above the joy that kids seem to derive from destroying things (like my house), hammering actually tests hand-eye coordination, visual-spatial skills and cause and effect. But mainly it's just plain fun. For older children, we have even used pasta (which is harder to pound).

**What you need...**

- Crunchy cereal
- Plastic tub
- Toy hammer, potato masher, soft meat tenderiser or some other implement for hammering.

# STACKING BLOCKS

*If you don't have nesting blocks, then find some cardboard boxes of different sizes that can fit into each other.*

**Handy Hint**

Make sure that you have enough blocks that they will tower to just over your standing baby's height! This helps get them up and moving, and they love running into it and knocking it down!

**What you need...**

- A variety of sizes of cardboard boxes

Whilst seemingly a simple activity, nesting blocks are a classic activity that provides many developmental benefits, such as development of fine-motor skills (starting with larger shapes and then progressing to handling smaller items) as well as spatial perception and sequencing. Start with something small like a tomato paste box, then perhaps a small cereal box, a shoe box, a large cereal box and then a packing box. Cut off the top flaps so that they easily nest in each other.

# PAINT SENSORY BAGS

*Want to be that cool mum that lets them paint but cannot handle the thought of the mess? Place paint in a sealed bag (such as a ziplock bag with extra taping on the seal), and let them mush the paint around to their hearts' content.*

**Handy Hint**

Place the bag on a white surface or piece of paper, or tape them on the window and encourage the kids to draw pictures with their fingers (or for older kids, encourage them to write their initials).

This activity is one of exploration and sensory play for younger children. They learn cause and effect as well as fine-motor skills. There are several variations that you can do with this activity.
For example:

- Put two separate colours in the bags, and let your kids push them around and around to explore colour mixing.
- Grab some writing tools, such as cotton tips or ice-cream sticks, and let them create shapes.

**What you need...**

- Plastic sandwich bags
- Paint
- Tape
- Optional: writing tools, like cotton tips, ice-cream sticks, etc.

# BANDED TUBE

1 – 2 years

*Grab a long cardboard tube, place all those hair ties that you have lying around the house around it and let your children explore.*

**Handy Hint**

As always, this activity requires constant supervision. Aim to use hair ties with a little less stretch in them so that they don't snap back much if tested.

**What you need...**

- Long cardboard tube (such as that from a finished roll of cling film)
- Hair ties

At first, I just let my daughter explore this activity. She started pulling on the individual bands and then tried to pull them off. This activity tests their fine-motor skills, and they need to be proficient at pincer grasping and dexterity. Being younger, I made sure that the bands weren't stretched on (they sat loosely) so that they could come off relatively easily. However, my son wanted to have a go, so I increased the degree of difficulty for him. Once they are off, the second activity is to try and put them back on, which requires a lot of practice. This is one of those great activities to whip out for your child in the high chair whilst you are making dinner (and supervising them, of course).

# COTTON WOOL BALL RACE

2 – 5 years

*This is a variation on the traditional egg and spoon race. Simply use a spoon and a cotton wool ball to have a race across the room.*

**Handy Hint**

Once your kids have mastered the skill, up the ante by creating an obstacle course with furniture and other items for them to navigate around whilst balancing the ball.

Cotton wool balls can easily fly off if kids aren't careful and patient. This is a true example of the tortoise and the hare. This activity enhances motor skills as well as problem-solving, coordination and balance.

**What you need...**

- Spoons
- Cotton wool ball (Or go ahead and be brave with a real egg!)

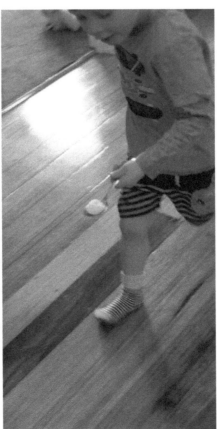

# BUILD YOUR OWN TRACK

*Got a heap of cars but nowhere for them to drive? Masking tape can create a perfect road map and gives you the flexibility to even go up vertical slopes (like the side of the couch) for added amusement!*

Both my boy and girl love playing with cars. But did you know that they are actually learning about the world around them whilst they play? Yes, this helps with their gross and fine-motor skills and cause-and-effect skills. However, they typically practise their language skills and learn concepts such as fast/slow, stop/go, up/down, and you can even introduce road rules.

**What you need...**

- Masking tape
- Little cars
- Blocks (optional)

## Handy Hint

We got out our blocks at the same time and made a little city around all the roads that we built, including fire stations, police stations and even a jail.

# JUMPING JACK

**What you need...**

- Tape

*What kid doesn't love to hop around? Simply tape lines to the floor and have them jump over them.*

A great activity for burning energy, this also enhances gross-motor skills and coordination.

You can also try the following:

- Hop over each line on one leg.
- Hop backwards over them.
- Long jump: How many lines can they jump over in one go?
- Run and jump: Experiment with how much farther they can jump with a running head start.
- Balancing beam: Take the tightrope challenge and try to walk along the line, and then jump to the next one.
- Put your feet on one end: How far can you stretch and reach?

Kids love a competition. Let them try to beat their previous score or, our favourite, beat their brother/sister. Let them experiment by creating different rules. How about the teddy doing a long jump or hopping with your eyes closed?

**Handy Hint**

As an extension activity for 3-5 year olds, try putting different numbers, letters or shapes on the floor and creating rules, such as 'Hop between the L and the R' or 'Crawl backwards to the triangle'.

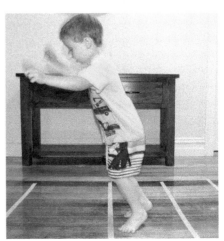

# BALLOON GAMES - ADVANCED

*For older children, there are still so many games that you can play with balloons that keep them moving and practising a variety of skills. Think of pretty much any ball game around, and I am sure you will find a balloon equivalent.*

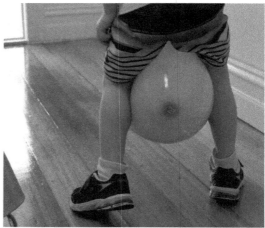

As with our basic activities, playing with balloons increases hand-eye coordination and gross-motor skills. When you are stuck indoors all day with a sporty child, create a balloon variation. Here are a number of ideas to help challenge your older child:

1. Have them place it between their legs and do a penguin waddle, without dropping it, around obstacles.
2. Blow the balloon along the ground around obstacles.
3. Have them balance the balloon on the back of their hand, and see how long they can do it.
4. Balloon tennis with wooden spoons. You can even create a net between two chairs with string or by pushing the chairs up against each other. (NB: this is really good for under 5's because the balloon moves slowly, allowing greater reaction time.)
5. Have them balance the balloon on their foot whilst lying down and having their feet in the air (great for core)
6. Play balloon hockey with a safe stick, such as a duster, and into an open box or laundry basket.

**REMEMBER, BURST BALLOONS CAN BE A SERIOUS CHOKING HAZARD. FOR YOUNG KIDS, THEY MUST BE SUPERVISED DURING THESE ACTIVITIES AT ALL TIMES.**

**What you need...**

- Balloons
- Optional: fly swats, bats, string, laundry basket

# INDOOR CROQUET

*Tape some paper tunnels to the floor, get a plastic golf club or pool noodle as a mallet and hit a ping-pong ball through the tunnels.*

**What you need...**

- Paper
- Tape
- Small ball
- Plastic golf club or other indoor-approved stick

Indoor sports games are Master 4's favourite. These types of games usually involve gross-motor skills, concentration and coordination all in one go.
Just don't expect that the rules will be adhered to; this ends up being a hybrid of croquet and golf!

**Handy Hint**

Increase the energy consumption by adding an activity that must be undertaken when the ball goes through the tunnel. For example, do 10 star jumps.

# POTATO WALK

*Simply put a potato between your legs, race to a finish line and try to drop it into a bucket. Then come back and get another and repeat. If the potato is dropped along the way, return to the starting line and try again.*

**What you need...**

- Potatoes (or apples, or oranges etc)
- Bucket

**Handy Hint**
Be sure to have a stack of potatoes for each child at the starting line. The first child to get them all in the bucket at the end wins.

This is a good activity for gross-motor skills, balance and energy consumption. I also like the element of problem-solving and the fact that it doesn't just rely on speed to win!

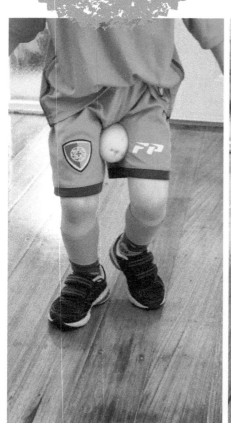

# SLIDE

*Create a slide by resting your cot or bed mattress on an incline from the couch or even by placing an opened large cardboard box on the bottom of the stairs.*

**Handy Hint**
Add a pillow on the bottom for a soft landing.

This is a simple activity, but I am sure that you can see the fun in it.
Please remember that this activity requires constant adult supervision and that you need to assess the safety aspects of your unique scenario.
Be conscious of the slope that you create and the suitability for your child.
Always keep a hand on the top of the mattress, or tape the top of the cardboard box on the stairs to prevent it from slipping.

**What you need...**

- Mattress or a cardboard box

# A-MAZE-ING

*Create a maze with books on the floor and let your child find their way out!*

**What you need...**

- Books

**Handy Hint**

If your child needs a bit of assistance, you could always leave a trail through the maze. Perhaps something messy like oats will do. Or you can dot some cars periodically along the route.

Have you ever seen those older men in the park playing with a giant chessboard? The creation of a human-sized maze is just as engaging and fun for children. Mazes enhance spatial awareness, problem-solving, patience, memory and, in this instance, gross-motor skills.

If you really can't contemplate the thought of pulling all the books down, you can create a cotton bud maze on the table for your figurines or consider making the maze with boxes or plastic containers.

# MINI GOLF

*If you have mini golf putters, you can create a mini target inside to practise putting. Or if you don't have a golf putter, a pool noodle or even a duster is a good substitute.*

Gross-motor skills, concentration, spatial perception and hand-eye coordination are just some of the skills that sports such as these foster. But really, it's just good ole fun. If you have the perseverance to make a 9-hole putting course, you will be rewarded with an afternoon's worth of entertainment. Of course, you could always combine this with an arts and crafts activity to get the kids involved in its construction.

**Handy Hint**
You can get really creative with a whole indoor golf course made out of cardboard boxes and tubes. See images for inspiration that will entice golfing parents to join in the fun!

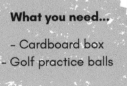

**What you need...**

- Cardboard box
- Golf practice balls

# RED LIGHT, GREEN LIGHT

3 – 5 years

*Remember this one from the school yard? Appoint one policeman with his back to everyone else on the starting line. When the policeman says, 'Green light!', everyone races until the policeman turns back around and shouts, 'Red light!'. If they catch anyone still moving, they are out. The objective is to catch the policeman.*

**Handy Hint**

You can make variations of this game with other coloured lights. For example, yellow light could signal crawling like a tiger and pink light could signal hopping.

This activity teaches children about games, taking turns and following directions. There is an element of problem-solving as kids learn the hard way that if you are moving too fast, it is very difficult to stop quickly (again, the tortoise and the hare).

**What you need...**

- Nothing

# SIMON SAYS

*We all know the game. Let one player take the role of Simon and provide instructions to other players. However, the only instructions that should be acted upon are those that start with 'Simon says'.*

Very much like Red Light, Green Light, this game teaches children about games, taking turns and following directions.

If you are having great success, try adding in a cleaning instruction now and then (like 'Simon says put your book back on the shelf') to achieve some other household objectives!

**Handy Hint**

Make sure to have silly and large movements in Simon Says to get maximum energy consumption!

**What you need...**

- Nothing

# WE'RE GOING ON A BEAR HUNT

*Hide a bear around the house, and go on a hunt to find it using directions like 'hot' and 'cold' as they go.*

**Handy Hint**

You could use a blue sheet for a river, a green sheet for grass, a sheet hung over some chairs for a cave and perhaps you could also play the 'We're going on a bear hunt' song at the same time!

**What you need...**

– A teddy bear

We got this idea after reading a book with the same name. It was a great way to inject some excitement and burn off some energy on a cold day.

# MUSICAL CHAIRS/LETTERS

*Here's another classic game. Place one less chair in the room than there are kids, and play some music. When the music stops, everyone needs to sit on a chair. The person left without a chair is out. Remove a chair and play again until only one person remains.*

**Handy Hint**

We all know this classic game, but you could also make a variation of this game for little kids or a small number of children. For example, place paper around the room with different colours, animals or letters on them. When the music stops, yell out one of the categories and everyone needs to race to that sign. In this instance, there are no kids getting out. But you could tally the winner in each round if your child desires a competition!

This activity teaches children about games, taking turns and following directions.

**What you need...**

- Chairs/cushions
- Paper (optional)

# WATER PLAY – ADVANCED

*Grab funnels, hoses, tubes, basically anything that you can find, and make an interactive water centre that will increase your child's STEM (science, technology, engineering and maths) learning and keep them entertained for hours.*

**Handy Hint**

With some of these, it is a little difficult to keep the water play contained in the house. If it's an indoor day, consider utilising a front or back porch if you can. Alternatively, you can use the shower or bath area.

I cannot think of a more engaging activity than water play for kids.
And did you know that the benefits of water play are immense? They develop motor skills (with actions such as pouring, squeezing, stirring), problem-solving skills, language development and STEM learning (like the way that liquids move, concepts such as full and empty, volume and motion, etc.).
I have attached a few images here to provide some inspiration, but it really comes down to what you have to use. If you can make a water wheel too, I HIGHLY recommend it!

**Note: Please remember that children must be constantly supervised when playing with water.**

**What you need...**

- An assortment of pipes, funnels, bottles, containers and buckets

# PATTERN PLAY

*Draw a pattern on a piece of paper, and have your child decorate it with items such as buttons or pasta.*

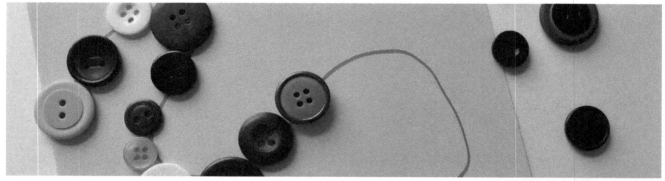

**Handy Hint**
If you are using coloured buttons, see if your child can replicate a pattern, such as red, green, blue, red, green, blue, etc. along the design.

A quiet activity, this one is all about concentration and control. It helps to develop fine-motor skills, hand-eye coordination, maths (patterns) and creativity.

**Note: Buttons and dried pasta can pose a choking hazard. Please maintain constant supervision of children whilst undertaking this activity.**

**What you need...**

- Paper
- Small items, such as buttons or pasta

# SOAP RACES

*Grab a piece of plastic guttering, wet it, and create your own soap races.*

Essentially, you need a smooth channel on which to conduct this. A piece of plastic guttering is perfect, but we have also improvised with a trestle table on one set of legs or even an opened cardboard box lined with plastic film.

If it is an indoor day, I recommend conducting this in the bath or shower to limit the amount of destruction. Make sure that the 'slide' and soap is wet. You can even put flags on them with toothpicks to tell the soaps apart.

Experiment with channel slopes, the level of water on the channel, etc. to see what works best. This is a great activity for motor skills (try holding that slippery sucker), cause and effect and STEM.

**Handy Hint**
You can carve the boats to make them more unique and to see whether this improves their handling ability!

**What you need...**
- Soap
- Plastic guttering (or any other long piece of plastic)

# CARDBOARD TUBE CRAFTS

*There are so many things that you can do with a cardboard tube. And if your family is like mine, they seem to accumulate them! Here is some inspiration to spark your imagination.*

**Handy Hint**

We always like to create something that enhances our play with other toys, such as a little rocket or racing cars in to which our smaller figurines can fit. However, this has admittedly led to tubes now remaining in our lounge room for weeks. (Well, I see tubes, but my kids see rockets.)

Arts and crafts have a number of benefits, such as the practice of fine-motor skills, patience, self-control, bonding and improved coordination. Combine that with the benefits of imaginative play, such as understanding the adult world, and those meagre tubes take on an entirely new meaning!

**What you need...**

- Cardboard tubes
- A variety of craft items, such as paints, coloured paper or string

# SPIDERWEB TARGETS

*Stick some tape to a door frame in a web with the sticky side out. Then create some newspaper balls and start throwing!*

**Handy Hint**

Master 4 is obsessed with Spiderman. So one night I set this up after he had gone to bed, and in the morning he was amazed that Spiderman had paid our house a visit!

This activity involves a lot of experimentation. How hard do I need to throw the ball in order to reach the target? How many stick? How close do I need to get? Of course, there is also the element of competition. Whilst improving coordination and motor skills, this activity also requires concentration and patience.

**What you need...**

- Masking tape that is quite sticky
- Paper

# MAGNETIC EXPLORATION

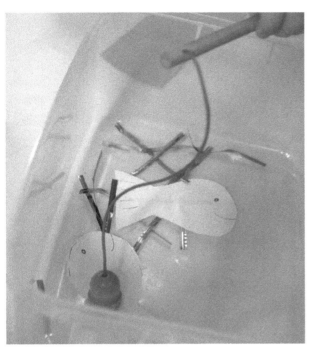

*So…. did you know that pipe cleaners are actually magnetic?! BLEW. MY. MIND. Grab a pile of pipe cleaners, a magnet and an empty container. Let your child explore by picking up the pipe cleaners with the magnet and transferring them to the container.*

This quiet activity helps children with hand-eye coordination, dexterity and concentration.

You can also cut the pipe cleaner into shorter lengths and place them in a bottle. Then using the magnet on the outside of the bottle, try and lift the pieces up. Hours' worth of mesmerising and strangely soothing play for you, I mean… your child.

Or you could even go fishing. Tape segments of pipe cleaners on the back of paper cut into the shape of fish, and place them into a container. Then tie the magnet to a piece of string and start fishing! We actually love to use our bath for our fishing adventures (with or without water).

**What you need...**

- Pipe cleaners (or those metal ties from freezer bags)
- A magnet

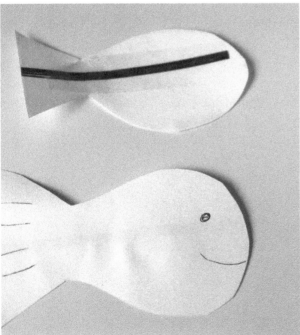

### Handy Hint

Show your child what happens if you use the magnet at one end of the pipe cleaner. When you get the pipe cleaner to stand up on end on the table, the look on their face will be one of pure amazement.

# PRETEND PLAY ADVENTURES

*OK, so I can't begin to list every pretend play adventure that you could do in your home here. So I won't. Please refer to pictures for inspiration.*

Whilst the nature of pretend play involves imagination and creativity, there are already so many toy companies that capitalise on this. The reality is that there is so much more you could do with your household items than you (or I, at least) ever expected.

Please refer to our inspiration gallery for precisely that.

**What you need...**

- Various household items
- A whole heap of imagination

**Below and Top Right:** Shoe shop
**Bottom Right:** Storytime at the Library

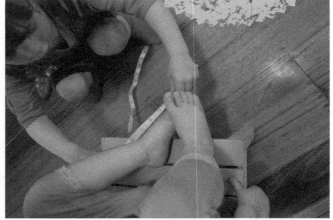

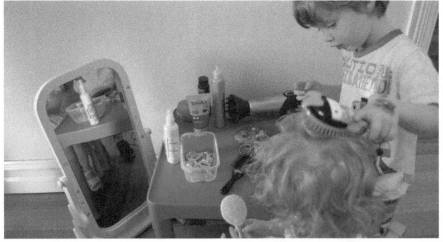
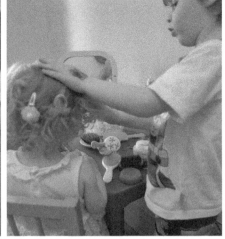

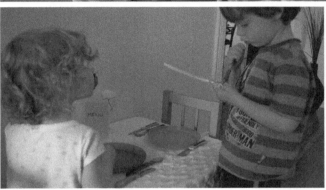

**Top Row:** Hairdresser

**Second Row:** Restaurant

**Below and Right:** Supermarket with scales and scanner (use a remote or any other rectangular item you can find!)

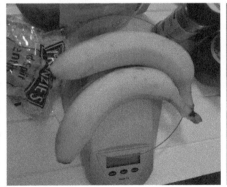

### Handy Hint

Be sure to join in on the fun with your child. Try to follow their lead, but be sure to reinforce social skills, like waiting, asking questions, being polite, etc. I was amazed at the terminology my son came up with as a shopkeeper. It really demonstrated that he has been observing interactions this whole time!

# COLANDER THREAD

*Get some pipe cleaners or toothpicks, and let your child practise threading them into the holes of a colander.*

**Handy Hint**

This requires a lot of practice for the pre-3s. I like to put one end into a hole and let them bend the other end in so that when they are not successful I don't have to keep picking up pipe cleaners.

**What you need...**

- Colander
- Pipe cleaners

This activity is all about concentration and improving hand-eye coordination, fine-motor skills and patience.

This is a typical activity that I whip out when I have Little Miss in the high chair as I'm cooking dinner. Of course, please be conscious of the size of the pipecleaners or toothpicks, and make your own decision on whether these are safe and suitable for your own child.

# AIRPORT AND CAR PARK

*Draw a runway on the lid of a pizza box, place your Christmas lights inside the box, poke the lights up and out of the lid and light up the runway! Or with the aid of a few cardboard tubes, convert a cereal box to a multi-level carpark.*

**Handy Hint**

Tape a cardboard tube to the lid and a small tub on the top and you have a helipad or airport control centre.

Are you sick of buying those add-on toys that all toy companies seem to want you to buy? This is a great activity to pair with the existing cars and planes that you already have. Of course, it could always be a racing car track rather than a runway, such is the power of imagination.

We also converted a cereal box and cardboard tubes to a multi-level carpark with off ramp.

In addition to fine-motor skill development, this activity provides imaginative play activities for your child to learn about the world around them.

**What you need...**

- Pizza box
- Christmas lights
- Small planes
- Black paper
- White crayon

# GEOGRAPHY IN A BOX

*Use a series of nested storage containers to help your child learn their place in the world.*

If your children are anything like my son, they are inquisitive about their place in the world and struggle with how their house number, street, suburb, city, state, country, continent and world fit into place.

I came across this idea and it was perfect to help my son understand these concepts. Of course, for a non-reader, I needed to put a series of visuals on the front of the boxes and then explain what each one was, but he is slowly grasping it.

**Handy Hint**

Whilst I try to avoid too much screen time (let's not pretend, it's a necessity sometimes), I sometimes give my phone to my son in the car so that he can watch the dot move on the maps app as we are driving.

He is actually very intrigued with where we are going; not only is he getting some spatial awareness of where we reside (he zooms in and out as far as the global map), but he is also actually picking up map-reading skills and starting to direct me along the way when I have the route marked!

**What you need...**

- Storage containers
- Printed images of state, country, world, etc.

# COUNTRY IN A BOX

2 – 5 years

*Choose a country and fill a box with items from that country. Then learn about the sights, sounds and tastes of that country together.*

Every week, choose a country that you will focus on. Over the course of the week, research the culture of that country together. Ideas include:

- Look up what music the country plays, and play it whilst you are around the home.
- Is there a traditional dance to which you could learn simple moves?
- What kids games do they play? Can you play these games at home with the items that you have? How about sports?
- What does the flag look like? Create a craft activity around colouring in, painting or creating the flag out of pieces of coloured paper.
- What are some unique animals from the country?
- Are there any interesting facts about the country?
- Does it have a king or a queen?
- What kind of lives do the children lead? Think about how you can place your child in the shoes of a child living in that country.
- Most importantly, what kind of food do they eat?

Pick a traditional recipe to try out at home and spend an afternoon cooking. A great idea to end the week is to finish with a meal from the country whilst playing music and even dressing up if you can!

**Handy Hint**
Invest in a map of the world (or print one out), and place a sticker on each country that you visit along the way!

# SEWING

*Get yourself a bit of hessian or other cloth and thick woollen thread on a needle, and teach your child how to sew a pattern.*

**Handy Hint**

Using a marker, draw a pattern or picture on the burlap for your child to follow.

If you want an activity that advances motor skills, this is it! Designed for the older preschool child, this activity helps refine fine-motor skills, concentration, creativity and problem-solving. It is best if you can keep the material taut and with space underneath to make it easier for your child to thread. This can be achieved by taping each end to chairs with a gap between them.

**What you need...**

- Burlap, hessian or fabric (loose weave)
- Wool thread
- A large threading needle suitable for little fingers

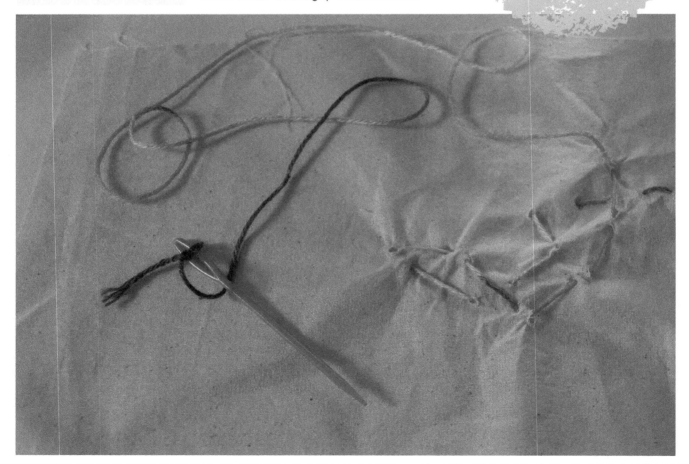

# ICE HOCKEY

*OK, this does require some foresight but not too much effort. Freeze a tub of water, place some blocks on either side as goals and play ice hockey with spoons and a bottle cap.*

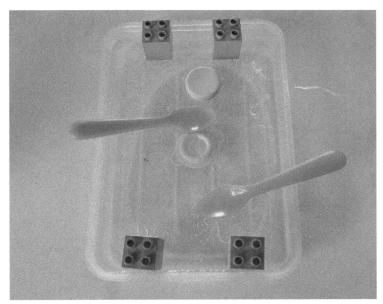

Don't let this game fool you. Despite being small, it is not necessarily quiet! Set the ground rules first, and then let your kids try and get a goal and navigate the other player's stick. Have shootouts. I don't know much about ice hockey, but it works and helps develop fine-motor skills and cooperation all at the same time!

## What you need...

- Container of ice
- Spoons
- Bottle caps
- Blocks (optional)

**Handy Hint**

If you are really clever, try freezing an egg ring (or something similar) into the centre of the container as the centre circle.

# CAR GARAGE

*Looking for a place to store all those cars and someone to throw out that growing mountain of cardboard tubes? Look no further than the car garage!*

**Handy Hint**

Do not use a container that you wish to reuse. We made this about 4 months ago, and I'm still not allowed to have my container back! On that note, if it's going to be a mainstay, I recommend taping the tubes together with masking tape prior to putting them into the container to secure them further.

A toy that also helps with storage? I'm in love. Whilst you wouldn't necessarily think of this as an activity, my son clocked up hours storing away his cars, bringing them out and putting them back in different orders.

**What you need...**

- Box, crate or container
- Many, many cardboard tubes
- Masking tape, printed signage (optional)

# ANIMAL CHARADES

*Take turns picking out an animal from a container, and act it out for the audience to guess.*

**What you need...**

- Container
- Pictures of animals

**Handy Hint**

Unlike traditional charades, you can use noises for the kids (particularly for the littlies) to help convey the animal.

This activity teaches children about games, taking turns and following directions. Most importantly, it's a great laugh for all.

If they've mastered the animals, you could always try professions (think chef, policeman, acrobat, gardener, etc.).

# MILK JUG TOSS

*Cut the bottom of a milk or juice container, and cover the cut edge with tape. Create a simple pompom with pieces of yarn and tie it to the handle of the milk jug. Swing the pompom up and try to catch it in the jug.*

**Handy Hint**

Be sure to make the length of the yarn appropriate for your child. The longer the yarn, the more swing it has to it and the harder it is to catch.

**What you need...**

- Milk jug
- Tape
- Yarn

This activity is great for hand-eye coordination, problem-solving and motor skills. It will take a little bit of practice to master but will provide a lot of entertainment along the way.

# FREEING THE ANIMALS

2 – 5 years

*OK, so this activity requires a little bit of foresight, but basically you gather up those farmyard animals and dinosaurs that you keep stepping on all over the house and freeze them in little tubs of water overnight. Provide your child with a variety of methods to free the animals to see which one works.*

This activity requires patience and problem-solving skills. At first, my kids tried bashing the ice with a spoon and knife. When that didn't work, they got the squeeze bottles and tried to squirt the ice with water, and then they sprinkled some salt on top. Slowly but surely they honed their technique and started freeing more and more animals with a high five each time.

Engage your children and ask them questions like, 'What happens when...', or, 'What do you think would happen if we...'. Try hot water versus cold water and see if there is any significant difference in the outcome.

### What you need...

- Containers of water
- Little animals or dinosaurs
- Squeeze bottles of coloured water
- Spoons and blunt knives (or other safe items to with which break ice)
- Salt

### Handy Hint

If you take this activity to the shower, you could hold the showerhead and run hot water on each of the ice moulds to free the animals.

Another idea is to freeze the animals in one big mixing bowl in layers. Add in some plastic greenery, and it makes for a beautiful exploratory piece.

# SCAVENGER HUNT

*Tape images of various items to collect on top of an egg carton and start finding.*

**What you need...**

- Egg carton
- A variety of items to hide around the house and pictures to match those items

**Handy Hint**

If you can get outside, create a nature scavenger hunt. If you can't, then hunt for items around the home (things like a button, hair clip, paper clip, elastic band, etc.). Or to make it a little easier, colour in each compartment of the egg carton with a different colour and ask your child to find an item around the house that matches each colour.

Scavenger hunts are just another way to build children's problem-solving skills and provide mental and physical exercise. When working together, it also teaches them about teamwork. This is a fun activity for around the home, but be sure to tailor it to your child.

For example, if I make things too hard, my son will give up early. I sometimes even add an item that I've been looking for. Currently, it's a mini Batman that's gone AWOL.

The egg carton is not a necessity, but it provides a neat container to collect their goodies. This is for the older age group. Please ensure supervision at all times so that younger children are not exposed to choking hazards.

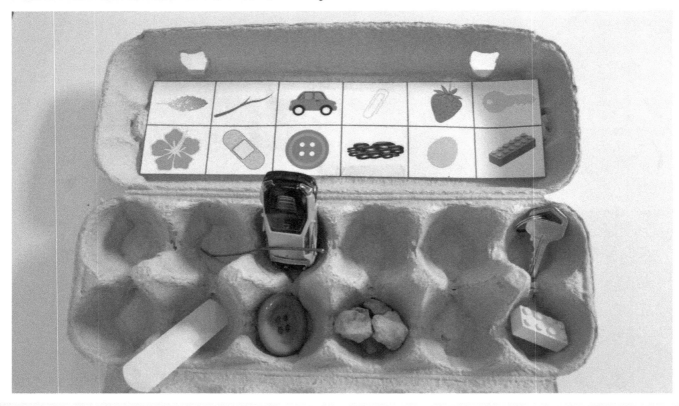

# SPONGE BALLS

*Cut a sponge into fingers and tie with string to create a bunch of sponge balls for indoor play or water play.*

**Handy Hint**

These can be used wet or dry. They can be used indoors as a soft ball for a bunch of throwing and catching activities.

Ball sports help hand-eye coordination as well as motor skills. You can use these balls indoor for throwing at targets or to each other. But they are definitely popular when wet during hot days on the front or back porch (or, of course, in the bath).

**What you need...**

- Sponges
- String

# TARGET PRACTICE

*Create some hanging targets with disposable cups hung on string from a cardboard box. Give your child a soft ball, position them a short distance away and let them shoot.*

**Handy Hint**

You can use the sponge balls on page 143 for this activity. Also, add colours, shapes or even letters on the cups, and ask your child to say which one they are aiming for in advance.

**What you need...**

- Soft ball
- Large cardboard box
- Disposable cups (or other hanging targets)
- String

This activity is good for colour recognition and hand-eye coordination. It also requires patience and perseverance, so be encouraging.

For my son, it has taken him a while to understand that you need to practice to become proficient at things, so we encourage him to keep going. At the same time, we also point out when we are having difficulties with something ourselves (like when I cook and mess up the dish...always).

# TODDLER PUZZLES

*Grab some ice-cream sticks, and butt them together then stick a photo on or do a drawing. Separate them, and let your toddler piece it back together.*

**Handy Hint**

When you put the sticks next to each other, tape a piece of masking tape on the back to secure them then put your design on the front. Once finished, remove the tape, cut between the sticks (if you have used a photo) and away you go.

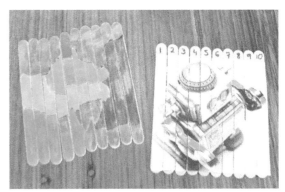

Puzzles benefit children in many different ways: problem-solving, literacy and numeracy and fine-motor skills, to name a few. But we always struggle to provide new and interesting puzzles for our children. This activity allows you to customise a puzzle to their interests, particularly when using photos that are familiar to them. You can also add numbers to the top of the ice-cream sticks to aid in developing early numeracy skills.

**What you need...**

- Approximately 10 ice-cream sticks
- A photo or textas to draw an image
- Glue and scissors (if using a photo)

# OFFICE WORK

*Create a laptop from an egg carton by cutting the lid off and taping it on the other way so that your child can pretend they are doing office work. Or you can use a notepad that has been folded out to create a laptop or even a piece of cardboard covered in foil.*

**Handy Hint**
Why not combine this into an 'office' pretend play scene.

OK, you probably think I am mad right about now! But one day after work, Master 3 (at the time) decided he wanted to do office work as well (poor misguided soul). Anyway, we grabbed an egg carton and cut off the lid so that the base could be flipped over to form keys, and then we taped the two pieces back together. I didn't even bother marking it to look like a laptop. That egg carton stayed in our lounge room for 6 months! Eventually, I had to throw it out because it was tattered, but Master 3 brought it out every day to sit on the couch and do some work.

My next creation was a little more refined; it had some aluminium foil on cardboard, a picture pasted on it for a screen and some letters written on the keypad. It truly is the simplest of things...

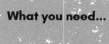

**What you need...**

- Egg carton
- Markers to draw a screen and keypad (optional)

# PUZZLE WALK

2 – 5 years

*Get your children to do puzzles with a twist... walking on their hands and fetching pieces from around the room.*

**Handy Hint**
Make sure they return the pieces one by one to maximise the energy burnt!

This is great for strengthening the upper body, improving gross and fine-motor skills and problem-solving. It adds a greater degree of difficulty to the puzzles that they may have previously mastered and allows for some energy to be burnt off.

**What you need...**
- Puzzles

# BEAN SCOOP

*Provide separate bowls of a variety of different dry beans and lentils, and let them use scoops or spoons to transfer to an ice cube tray.*

**Handy Hint**

If your child is still sticking objects in their mouth, try edible items. Depending on your child's age, this could include chickpeas, sultanas, dried fruit, grated carrot or cheese, red kidney beans and other cooked beans.

This activity assists with fine-motor skills as well as hand-eye coordination and problem-solving. Note that this activity cannot be undertaken until children are beyond sticking everything in their mouth. Unless, of course, you make sure that it is cooked food. It may end up being mushier, but c'est la vie!

**What you need...**

- Beans
- Scoops or spoons
- Ice cube tray

# ALPHABET THROW

*This one is for your budding spellers. Attach sticky notes on a wall with one letter on each note. Roll up a pair of socks, ask your child to stand behind a line, call out a letter and ask them to try and hit it.*

**Handy Hint**
Start off easily with just the letters of your child's name on the wall then expand as their alphabet grows, trying to keep a letter or two ahead.

**What you need...**

- Sticky notes
- A pair of socks

This is simply a way to combine learning our alphabet with learning hand-eye coordination skills.

For sports or competition-obsessed kids, this is a great and slightly different way to encourage alphabet practice.

Sometimes we even say that you have to 'bop' the letter with the socks and then run a loop of the house before the next letter, to burn off more energy.

# BALL CATCH

*Have each person hold a plastic cup and stand reasonably close together. Toss a small ball (e.g., a ping-pong ball) to each other and catch it in your cup.*

**Handy Hint**

Combine this activity with a few other sports (such as mini golf on page 117 and ice hockey on page 137) to create your own indoor Olympics on a rainy day.

If you are looking for a less nerve-wracking indoor ball sport than those that use a large ball around all your belongings, this is it. My son has little to no concentration span, but bring out a ball sport like this and he is hooked!
Start the game relatively close together and increase the distance as their proficiency increases. This activity increases their overall coordination, hand-eye coordination and gross-motor skills.

**What you need...**

- Plastic cups
- Small plastic ball

# ACTIVE ALPHABET

*Simply pick a card at random, ask your child to sound out the letter and then do the activity.*

**Handy Hint**

When establishing the cards, concentrate on achieving a balance of the three fitness elements: endurance, strength and flexibility.

**What you need...**

- DIY exercise alphabet cards

Looking for a way to really burn off that indoor energy in an educational way? Try creating an exercise for every letter of the alphabet!

We all know the benefits of exercise for kids and adults alike, so it's a great idea to burn off some energy whilst practising the alphabet.

# MOVEMENT MEMORIES

*This is a game for more than one. Get one child to do a movement (think jumping three times or hopping twice or acting like a frog), and then the next person has to repeat that movement and add one of their own. The last person standing who doesn't forget a movement is the winner.*

**Handy Hint**

Try to make some of the movements about space. So perhaps hop in the corner of the rug, run from the lounge to the kitchen or jump from the bottom stair to the floor. For more visual people, providing unique spaces for each activity will help them remember.

**What you need...**

- Your imagination

This is a good game to get the wiggles out as well as exercise the memory. Whilst it is great to include a vast array of energetic activities, change the tone every now and then by pretending to be an alligator or slithering like a snake! You can also create a natural rhythm to the game and aid in memory retention by referring to the first activity as 'do 1...', the second as 'do 2...' and so forth.

# SACK RACES

*Bring back that old-school classic with some pillow cases.*

**Handy Hint**

Traditionally, this is a game for more than one child. But you could create an obstacle course for one. I like to time it (or pretend to, at least) and then encourage them to do it over and over again to beat their time.

Don't underestimate how much energy this burns off! A great activity for balance, coordination and gross-motor skills, it is also a heap of fun, which is why it has lasted the test of time.

**What you need...**

- Pillow cases

# 3-LEGGED RACE

*Here's another classic for the older pre-schooler. Just line two children up next to each other, tie a stocking loosely around their joint middle leg, stand back and watch!*

**What you need...**

- Pantyhose or something to safely and gently tie legs together (i.e., a medical bandage, ribbon, etc.)

I am not sure there is an activity that promotes and requires teamwork more than this one. What better way to encourage sibling cooperation and problem-solving?

**Handy Hint**

OK, this may be a little controversial, but someone once told me that his punishment for fights was forcing his children to work together by walking three-legged for a specified period of time! Food for thought...

# STRAW BUILDINGS

*Straws can be used as great building materials to make exciting 3D shapes. Show your child how to place one end of a straw into another and bend it around in crazy shapes. See what they can come up with.*

**Handy Hint**

Cut holes in the middle of the straw by folding the straw over and then cutting a slit; this allows you to thread other straws through it.

Whilst clearly assisting with fine-motor skills, this activity also challenges kids to think creatively, solve problems and persevere. It also teaches the fundamentals of STEM. Your child is likely to need some assistance for a while, but this makes for a great indoor activity on a wet day. Think outside the box too. You can create some crazy things with straws: a hat, a roller coaster for a ping-pong ball, a house, etc.

**What you need...**

- Straws

# MARBLE TRACK RACES

*Cut a pool noodle in half. Sit the top of the two noodles at the edge of a table (tape it in place) and the bottom in a container. Then take a marble or ping-pong ball each and race them down the centre of the noodle.*

**Handy Hint**
Experiment with different angles by moving the container on the ground in and out to see how that affects the speed. (It is often good to keep one noodle half in the original position and the other in the modified position to compare speeds at the same time).

Yes, this activity explores concepts around gravity and physics and improves fine-motor skills. At the end of the day, it's the competition that had my son and his friend going for hours!

**What you need...**

- Pool noodle
- Marbles/ping-pong balls
- Shoebox

FINISH LINE

# CAR LAUNCHER

*Pull back a rubber band, place a small car in a box behind the line where the band was and let go!*

**Handy Hint**

You can also make a car launcher out of plastic guttering. And if you direct it off-centre into a tube, your car may go upside down. Try and experiment with curves to send your car in all directions.

**What you need...**

- Cardboard box
- 2 rubber bands

Coupled with my little boy's love of cars is his love of fast cars!
This car launcher provides introductory physics lessons in propulsion and force. Try experimenting with cars of different sizes, different forces or by launching onto different materials (such as carpet, tiles, etc.) to see what happens...

# MISSION IMPOSSIBLE

3 – 5 years

*Use a roll of string to create a spiderweb grid from one wall to another (or banister) by securing with tape, and then challenge your child to get through without falling over or touching the string!*

**Handy Hint**
Make sure that there is a lot of verticality in the game so that your child has to go over, crawl under and climb through at various points. But for beginners, you can create one line every 30 cm or so at varying heights.

**What you need...**

- String
- Tape

Quick story... my son had a friend over and his mum and I were so busy chatting we didn't notice the boys creating their 'parent trap' in the bedroom with the string from his kite! That got me thinking, what a wonderful web to try and crawl through. Clearly this is for older children and requires supervision, but it is a great way to test motor skills and problem-solving abilities. If you are creative and have the right space (i.e., say working off a banister on one side), it really doesn't take much sticky tape or time.

# TOY FLYING FOX

3 – 5 years

*String a line from a high point to a low point, clip a stuffed toy to a coat hanger and away you go!*

Good old plain racing fun will have your kids in giggles. A good activity to do with slightly older children is to experiment with the angle of the line and the weight or size of the stuffed toy.
Does it go faster or slower along the line? Or does it fall off completely?

**What you need...**

- Coat hanger with clips
- Small soft toy

**Handy Hint**
If you are having any friction issues that are causing the animal to go slowly, just add a little Vaseline® to the underside of the coat hook.

# ICY POLE WEAVE

*Secure two icy pole sticks together in a cross, find yourself some wool and start weaving.*

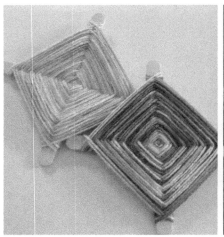  

**Handy Hint**

To brighten it up, try changing the colour of the wool halfway through or using two pieces of wool at the same time.

**What you need...**

- 2 icy pole sticks
- Wool in wonderful colours

Secure the start of the yarn in a knot at the centre of the icy pole cross, pull across to the next stick by crossing it over, come back around under and then continue to the next stick in sequence (refer to pictures).
This activity helps with concentration, creativity, fine-motor skills and imagination.

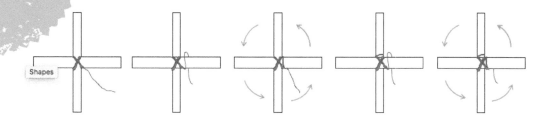

# SUMO DUDES

3 – 5 years

*We've all done this. Get two pillows per child, stuff one at the front and one at the back under a large T-shirt (adults size is perfect) and tie a belt around them if needed. Then let the games begin.*

If you have more than one child, particularly if you have boys, then you probably have experienced wrestling at some point or another. Let's turn that game into something fun, and let them get all that Wrestlemania out in a safe way. This burns so much energy because of the effort it takes them to get up off the ground!
Be sure to watch them constantly and to establish the rules that you need in order to keep it safe.

**Handy Hint**
Make a secured area that is free from the edges of furniture, and delineate it with cushions or a piece of tape on the ground.
That's really the main rule: Do not leave the safe zone!

**What you need...**

- Large T-shirts (perhaps Mum's or Dad's)
- Pillows
- Belt or rope

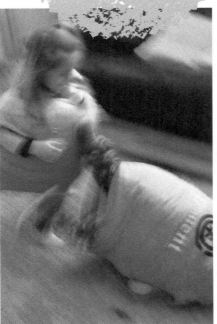

# TABLE BALL

*Each player has a cardboard tube and a ping-pong ball. The aim of this game is to blow the ball across a table and into a cup hanging from the edge. The winner is the one who gets the most balls in a cup from a set number.*

**Handy Hint**

If you don't have ping-pong balls, you could always try using cotton wool balls.

This game is a game of skill, perseverance, problem-solving and practice. Get two competitive souls next to each other, and they will be going at it for hours trying to perfect the art. This is a great game to add to any indoor Olympics theme.

**What you need...**

- Disposable cups
- 2 cardboard tubes each (e.g., from a roll of cling film)
- Ping-pong balls

# WEB RESCUE

*Grab a laundry basket and place some animals or objects in there that need rescuing. Create a spiderweb through the basket with some string (make sure to pull it tight and tie it off well to maintain tension), and then get your child to rescue the animals*

**Handy Hint**

Start off with smaller toys for younger kids and then 'trap' bigger toys as their skill level grows.

My little boy is so intrigued by spiderwebs and anything trapped in there. I made this game for both of my children, and whilst they are 2 years apart in age they both really enjoyed it. This game focuses on problem-solving and fine-motor skills; it took my youngest a few minutes of trial and error before rescuing her toys, but she had a lot of fun.

Please be sure to maintain constant supervision.

**What you need...**

- Laundry basket
- String
- A variety of soft toys

# PANTYHOSE BOWLING

*Grab a pair of your old pantyhose, cut off one full leg and put a ball in it. Tie it around your child's waist so that the ball is almost touching the ground, and then let them swing at targets, such as disposable cups or another ball.*

This is a great game of balance, coordination and gross-motor skills. Most importantly, it will keep children in stitches of laughter as it is just so different from their regular games.

You can switch it up by having a series of upturned cups that need to be knocked over or by having another ball/orange that they need to hit with their ball to move into a target (such as a laundry basket). If your child finds an orange or apple too heavy, try a lighter item such as a tennis ball.

**Handy Hint**

You can also create a new challenge by putting the open end of the stocking on your child's head like a beanie! Refer to photo below.

**What you need...**

- Pair of old pantyhose
- Ball, orange or other found object to put in stocking
- Plastic cups or other target

# PING-PONG SHOOTERS

*Cut the bottom of a cup (and tape the cut edge to prevent injury). Tie a knot in the balloon and cut the bottom from the balloon. Cover the larger end of the cup with the balloon and shoot pompoms (or ping-pong balls).*

**Handy Hint**

With any game like this, I like to make a target for kids to shoot at. I find as soon as anything becomes a competition, it lasts WAY longer. So, get an upturned container, laundry basket or piece of paper with a target on it, and let the competition begin.

Not only is this fun, but games such as this develop gross-motor skills and, in particular, hand-eye coordination. As children repeat the game, they experiment with different methods to hone their skills and increase their success rate.

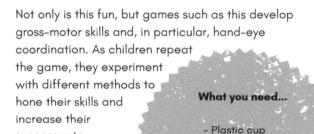

**What you need...**

- Plastic cup
- Balloons
- Ping-pong balls, pompoms or cotton wool balls
- Tape

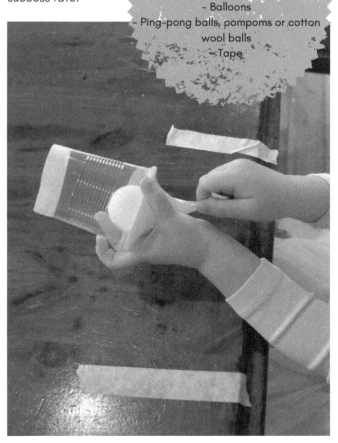

# MEMORISATION

*Put 5 objects on the floor and ask your child to memorise them. Then cover the objects with a blanket and take one object away whilst the child's eyes are closed. Uncover and test your kid's memory on which item is missing.*

**Handy Hint**
Keep the toys/objects relatively small so that your child cannot tell what you are taking!

**What you need...**

- 5 items
- Blanket or towel

This came from a friend of mine who has 3 boys with whom it is a hit. I tried it with Master 4, and the concentration from a boy with no concentration was amazing! This is a great activity to increase concentration span and maintain focus as well as challenge and train the brain.
I now conduct this activity regularly to provide Master 4 with some concentration activities. He loves to try to raise the bar each time, and we have increased to about 10 objects.

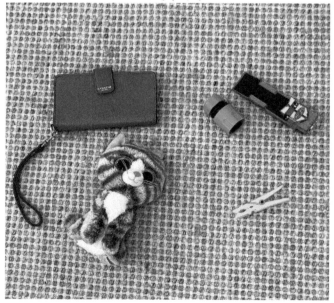

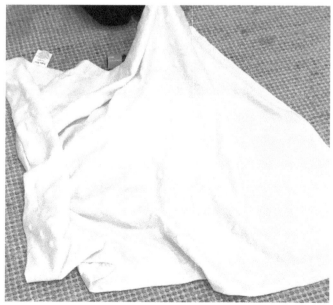

# BALL MAZE

*Get a large, shallow cardboard box and tape cardboard tubes or cardboard arches in there. Get a small ball or marble; the aim of this game is to move the box in a way that moves the ball through the tubes.*

**Handy Hint**

Depending on what you have, there are a variety of different materials that you can use. You can even create a 'false floor' insert such that there is a hole for the ball to drop into if it reaches the end of the course. Refer to photos for inspiration.

I think everyone had a small ball maze at one time or another when they were growing up. Well, this homemade version is made on a larger scale for smaller kids to aid in coordination, perseverance, and problem-solving.

Use what you have and make the rules up to suit. You can even set it up in a clear container with a lid so that the ball doesn't come out. We like to put a colour on the tubes or arches and then yell a colour out that our child then needs to aim for.

**What you need...**

- Cardboard box
- Cardboard tubes
- Small ball

# TODDLER
EXPERIMENTS

# CHAPTER
# SIX

# Experimental Learning...

On the following pages are some easy experiments to help teach your child about basic science and engineering concepts.

When undertaking these activities with your child, allow your child to lead inquiry and discovery.

At the start of the activity, ask your child questions like:

> 'What do you think will happen?'
>
> 'Why will it happen?'
>
> Allow your child to make observations.

At the end, the following questions can lead to further discussion, exploration and experimentation.

> 'What do you think happened?'
>
> 'Why did it happen?'
>
> 'What do you think would happen if we used X?' (Change one variable: for example, the material used.)

I have an inquisitive 4 year old and he LOVES asking 'Why?' for everything. After undertaking some of these experiments, he now asks to do more and more every time I ask him what he would like to do for the day.

# STRAW ROCKETS

*Colour in our rocket template and cut out all the parts. Wrap the rectangle loosely around a straw and secure with tape (so it is in the shape of a tube). Screw the end of the tube into a tip. Cut out the two rocket bodies and place on either side of the tube and secure together as shown. Place a straw in the bottom and blow into it to launch!*

**Handy Hint**

My son is obsessed with rockets and space. Here is a simple way to introduce engineering into the home and have heaps of fun in the process! Use our downloadable template as your guide. Experiment with the size of the fins, the angle of take-off (straight up, straight in front or something in between) and how hard you blow on the straw. This activity is great because it is effectively two activities: an arts and crafts activity and an experiment.

**What you need...**

- Straws
- Paper

**Kid-Friendly Explanation**

At the preschool stage, the STEM discussion may just be limited to propulsion; you need a lot of force to get a rocket to the moon! If you are really ambitious, try and discuss drag; the different shapes that you try will either increase or decrease the drag, holding your rocket back. We also recommend having a landing strip on the floor to measure who can launch their rocket the farthest!

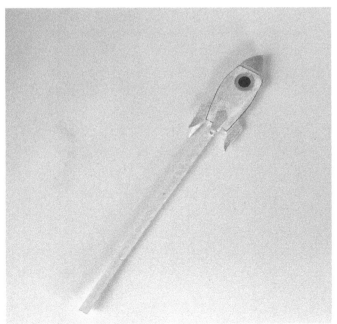

# EXPERIMENTING WITH AIR

*Place a drinking straw between 2 kitchen sponges in a ziplock bag. Seal the bag and tape along the edge. Press down on the sponge and watch the pompom fly across the table.*

**Handy Hint**

First off, you need to make sure that you have a good airtight seal, the exception being the straw. Then blow into the straw to provide more air in the bag and more impact when it moves.

While doing this experiment, you could also try blowing other objects across the table, some larger and heavier and some smaller. Which ones move? Which ones don't? Why do you think they didn't move?

If your children are becoming competent at moving the pompoms, you could even make this into a game with each child in which they are required to race their pompoms to a finish line.

**Kid-Friendly Explanation**

Air is a difficult thing to explain when you can't see it. Even more difficult is explaining that air is actually matter and takes up space.

For toddlers, explain that there is air in the bag. When we push down on the bag, we push the air out of the bag (through the straw). The air that you can feel blowing through the straw is that air that is being pushed out of the bag.

To aid in comprehension, you could do the exact same exercise with a liquid so that your child can understand that air is similar yet unseen.

**What you need...**

- Kitchen sponges
- Ziplock bag
- Straw
- Pompoms or cotton wool balls

# ENGINEERING BRIDGES

*This is a simple test of different bridge styles to see which one withstands the heaviest load. Use 2-3 blocks and stand them as columns, and then use strips of paper in different arrangements. Find something small (like cotton wool balls) to load them, and see which one can carry the most load (i.e., most number of cotton wool balls).*

**Kid-Friendly Explanation**

It is very difficult to explain to a toddler the principles of load transfer. I have settled for simply saying that when an object sits on a bridge, the load of the object needs to be transferred down to the ground. There are different types of structures that can be used for bridges, and they each transfer the load a different way, some more effectively than others.

**What you need...**

- Blocks
- Paper cut into lengths
- Something relatively light to test bridges with, such as cotton wool balls, stones, buttons, etc.

**Handy Hint**

Inevitably, my children wanted to use their bridges for something more exciting than cotton wool balls or little marbles. So we experimented with Lego men and little cars. If you have some thin cardboard on hand, replace the paper with the cardboard and experiment further with even larger objects. The winning bridge was then used as part of a race track for the rest of the day.

# WATER LIFE CYCLE

*Mark up a ziplock bag as demonstrated in the pictures. Now, warm up some water until steam starts to rise, add in some blue food colouring (optional) and put it in the ziplock bag. Then stick it on a window (preferably one in direct light) and watch the process.*

**Handy Hint**

As the water evaporates, the vapours will form at the top of the bag (i.e., like clouds forming in the atmosphere). Then water will start to appear on the bag and slide back down (i.e., rain), which will flow back to the 'sea' (the bottom of the bag).

This cycle may continue to reoccur if the weather allows (or if you blow on the 'sea' with a hairdryer; be sure not to melt the bag).

This is an activity that is particularly good for a hot day. Try starting by putting an ice block in the ziplock bag. This helps in demonstrating the solid state.

**Kid-Friendly Explanation**

Water can exist in 3 states; solid (like ice), liquid (like the water from the tap) and gas (like air). The way it changes between these different types is through heating and cooling.

When it is really, really cold, water is frozen. As it gets warmer, it melts and turns to a liquid. And when it gets really hot, it evaporates into a gas.

These changes happen the other way too (i.e., gas to liquid to solid as the water cools).

**What you need...**

- Ziplock bag
- Ice block or water
- Blue food colouring (optional)
- Permanent marker

# TORNADO IN A BOTTLE

*Fill a bottle with water and a very small drop of dishwashing liquid. Leave a little room at the top and put the lid on. Turn the jar upside down, shake it from side to side in a circular motion and watch the tornado form.*

**Handy Hint**

My kids loved adding glitter to the jar and watching it swirl around in the tornado. You could also experiment with different sized jars. We used a wider jar to create a much wider tornado.
And if you have very small figurines, why not see if you can get them moving in the tornado as well!

**What you need...**

- Clear jar (preferably plastic)
- Glitter (optional)
- Dishwashing liquid
- Water

**Kid-Friendly Explanation**

At this stage, I have elected to keep things super, super simple here as the creation of tornadoes are an incredibly complex phenomenon and very difficult to explain at the toddler level (I struggle to understand myself!)
So I have settled with the explanation that tornadoes are a violently rotating column of air that extend from the ground and are created under certain conditions.

# VOLCANOES

*Pour vinegar over baking soda. Easy!*

**Handy Hint**

If you pour vinegar over baking soda, you will get a reaction. I have seen many variations
of this volcano experiment, each quite impressive for children.
A few ideas:

- If you put a squirt of dishwashing liquid in with the vinegar, it will create a bigger and foamier reaction. And if you add colour, it makes it look a tad more awesome.
- Cut the core out of an apple and add in the baking soda. Pour over the vinegar.
- Cut a lemon in half and mush up the contents before adding the baking soda. In this one, you do not need vinegar; it is the citric acid in the lemon that reacts with baking soda. (Note: the reaction is a small fizzy one, not a massive bubbly one.)
- This is a favourite in our house; get a number of clear glass cups and put baking soda in the bottom of each along with a drop of different food colouring. Now pour vinegar over each one and watch them froth over.
- Another great idea is to put some baking soda in a bottle and bury it in a sandcastle. Now when you add the vinegar, it LOOKS like a volcano

**Kid-Friendly Explanation**

When vinegar and baking soda mix, they
undergo a reaction and make a gas (carbon
dioxide). What you are doing in this
experiment is watching the reaction occur
and the gas being released.

**What you need...**

- Baking Soda
- Vinegar
- Optional: dishwashing detergent,
food colouring, other items as per
variations listed.

# BUBBLE BUBBLE

2 – 5 years

*Mix 1 drop of food colouring with water in a clear glass and add oil. Allow everything to settle, and then drop an effervescent tablet in (e.g., Alka-Seltzer) and observe the reaction.*

### Kid-Friendly Explanation

The first concept is that water and oil do not mix; they don't like each other. The second concept is that an effervescent tablet and water react together to cause a bubbly gas (i.e., carbon dioxide). So, when the water starts bubbling, it shoots up through the oil (remember: they don't mix), creating the beautiful effect that we see.

### What you need...

- Food colouring
- Water
- Oil
- Alka-Seltzer tablet, or other effervescent tablet

### Handy Hint

The visual effect is the water bubbling through the oil. For this reason, I prefer 5 parts oil to 1 part water, which allows for a greater visual effect (i.e., the oil layer is large).

# FIREWORKS

2 – 5 years

*Fill a cup with warm water (approximately ¾ full). In a separate bowl put a little oil (say 1/8 cup) with drops of food colouring in it. Now pour the coloured oil gently into the cup and watch the effect.*

**Handy Hint**

We like to have a few different bowls of oil with different food colourings for extra effect.

**Kid-Friendly Explanation**

The first concept is that water and oil do not mix; they don't like each other. The second concept is that food colouring mixes with water; it loves water but doesn't love oil. So when you pour the food colouring or oil mix into the water, the food colouring moves to the water, which it loves, creating the fireworks that you see. You will notice if you watch long enough that it will mix with the water properly.

**What you need...**

- Clear cup
- Warm water
- Oil
- Food colouring

# HOT AND COLD AIR

*Put a balloon over the top of an empty 1.25 L soft drink bottle. Set up two bowls; one with warm tap water and the other with cold water (put some ice in it too). Now place the soft drink bottle in each container for a few minutes each, and observe what happens to the balloon.*

**Handy Hint**

My son was intrigued by this and then tested the bottles the other way; what happens if we move the bottle from warm to cold water (and vice versa).

**What you need...**

- Empty 1.25L soft drink bottle
- Balloon
- Containers of warm and cold water.

**Kid-Friendly Explanation**

The first concept to explain is that there is air inside the bottle but that it cannot escape as there are no holes. When the air becomes warm (i.e., it is placed in the warm water), it expands (or needs more space) and therefore stretches out the balloon. When the air gets cold, it contracts (or needs less space), so the balloon deflates. My son likes me explaining it as air being full of little particles. When the particles are cold, they huddle together (much like we would). And when they are warm, they want their space.

Please note that this experiment does not need to be done with boiling water. Be sure to monitor your child around water, particularly where warmer water is used.

# STATIC BUTTERFLY

*You know that shock that your child gets on the slide at the playground or from running around on the carpet? Well, here is a way to explore that concept further. Simply rub a balloon on a tissue paper butterfly and watch its wings flap.*

### Handy Hint

Create a butterfly like the one pictured using tissue paper and other craft items. Blow up a balloon and rub it in your hair to create an electric charge. Then hold it in front of the butterfly (making sure not to touch it), moving the balloon farther and closer, and watch the butterfly flap! Yep, the kids loved making the butterfly's wings move. But you know what was even more fun? Rubbing the balloon on your little sister's hair and watching it stand up in the air! H.I.L.A.R.I.O.U.S!

### Kid-Friendly Explanation

My child loves static electricity, from the carpet in our home to the slide at the playground. Every now and then he will get a shock that makes him giggle. But how do we explain this phenomenon?

This is a difficult one for preschoolers, and whilst not failproof, the best way that I have found to date is to explain the following three concepts:

1. Every item is made of tiny, tiny particles that contain energy.

2. When we rub one object against another (like a balloon against the tissue paper), one object passes on energy to another. As a result, it becomes charged, and the other item becomes the opposite charge.

3. Opposites attract, so this opposite charge in each item makes them want to stick together.

**What you need...**

- Tissue paper
- Balloon
- Arts and craft material to make the butterfly (optional)

# SHAVING FOAM CLOUDS

2 – 5 years

*Fill a jar with water almost to the top. Cover the top of the water with shaving cream. Fill up a dropper with coloured water and let your child start dropping on the cloud. After a while, when the 'cloud' gets too full it will start 'raining' into the water.*

**What you need...**
- Shaving cream
- Jar
- Water
- Food colouring
- A dropper

**Handy Hint**

This experiment is good to do in conjunction with the water life cycle experiment (refer to page 176) to further demonstrate the concept.

**Kid-Friendly Explanation**

As the sun comes out, it warms the water on the Earth, which then evaporates and rises, much like the steam that you see coming out of the kettle. As it rises, it cools down because of the temperature in the sky (it is colder in the sky), and so it condenses and forms clouds. Clouds are a collection of water droplets. When the clouds have so much water in them, they get too heavy and they drop the water (i.e., it rains).

# OIL AND WATER

*Make the coloured ice cubes in advance. Fill the bottom of a tray with oil and place the ice cubes in. As the ice begins to melt it will bead into the oil. Let your child swirl the cubes around to see what effects are made.*

**Handy Hint**

For an extra bit of fun, add glow-in-the-dark paint to the ice cubes and mix well before freezing. This packs an amazing wow factor into the experiment.

**What you need...**

- Oil (use vegetable oil, or baby oil only if your children will not eat it)
- Water
- Food colouring

**Kid-Friendly Explanation**

This is a simple case of demonstrating that water and oil do not like each other (i.e., they don't mix). You can also explain the concept that ice is water that is frozen (i.e., a solid). As it gets warmer, it melts (i.e., it becomes a liquid).

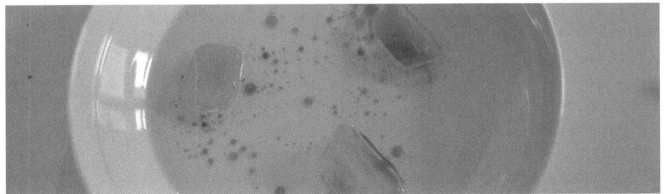

# BABY LAVA LAMPS

1 – 5 years

*In a ziplock bag, place oil (a clear oil is preferred) and water with some food colouring. Be sure to only fill the bag halfway. To give you an idea, I used 2 parts oil and 1 part water. Zip it up, seal it thoroughly with tape and let your baby explore.*

## Kid-Friendly Explanation

Much the same as the oil and water experiment on page 185, this is a simple case of demonstrating that water and oil do not mix.

## What you need...

- Ziplock bag
- Oil (use vegetable oil, or baby oil only if your children will not eat it)
- Water
- Food colouring

## Handy Hint

If you happen to have glow-in-the-dark paint, mix this with a little water and use in place of the coloured water. Your baby will get a kick out of this in the dark!

# MOUNTAINS

*Use some soggy biscuits to demonstrate the tectonic plates that are present on the earth's surface. Push them up against each other to demonstrate how mountains are made.*

**Handy Hint**

If the biscuits become too soggy in water, try just dipping in one edge of the biscuit (the sides that you will push against each other).

Alternatively, you can cover an upturned bowl with icing and place the biscuits on them to more accurately represent the Earth's surface.

**Kid-Friendly Explanation**

The Earth's crust is made of many plates sitting next to each other. These plates move as the result of activity below the Earth's surface. When they move against each other, it creates mountains. This process occurs very slowly.

You could also expand on this by highlighting the link between plate movements and earthquakes.

**What you need...**

- Biscuits
- Paper

# THE FLOWER FOOD

*Quite simply, add water and a drop or two of food colouring to each vase (or cup). Add one white flower to each vase, and let nature take its course. Make sure that the stem of the flower is freshly cut to allow faster water uptake.*

### Handy Hint

Different flowers absorb water at different rates. The experiment could take one night or many nights. Roses really work well (I was surprised to see colour occurring in a matter of minutes!) You can also use celery.

Once they are coloured, expand upon the experiment by exploring what happens if you move the roses to another colour. You will end up exploring primary colour mixing too.

### Kid-Friendly Explanation

Just like us, plants need water to survive. But plants drink their water from the soil; it travels through the roots and up its stem to the leaves and flowers. So when we put the cut flower in water, it starts drinking the water which travels up the stem and into the flower, causing it to change colour (due to the coloured water).

**What you need...**

- Water
- Vases
- Food Colouring
- White flowers

# FILL THE CUP

*Fill two cups up with coloured water, fold a piece of paper towel and connect to a third (middle) cup.*

**Handy Hint**

Make the two original cups of water different colours using food colouring. The middle cup will end up a mixture of the two.

**What you need...**

- 3 clear cups
- Paper towel

**Kid-Friendly Explanation**

Paper towels absorb water. When you place the paper towel in the water, it absorbs it slowly up the length of the paper towel and all the way to the empty cup!

# BALLOONING

*This is a DIY parachute. Just punch 4 holes slightly under the rim of a plastic cup, and tie 4 equal-sized pieces of string to the cup and the 4 corners of a nappy bag or handkerchief.*

**What you need...**

- Disposable plastic cups
- Disposable nappy bag
- String

**Handy Hint**

Drop these from a high place and watch them float to the ground. Test how it drops with something in the cup (like a peg). Then test what happens if you don't have the parachute.

**Kid-Friendly Explanation**

Gravity is a force that pulls objects to the ground. It's why an object falls when dropped and why we don't float away. When we use a parachute, this creates some air resistance, which slows the fall of the object.

# SWIRLY MILK

2 – 5 years

*Place milk in a shallow dish and then put a drop of food colouring in. Drop in some dishwashing liquid and watch the colours swirl.*

**Handy Hint**

Grab a toothpick and let your children gently swirl patterns in the milk. You can also give your children a paintbrush to dot the dishwashing liquid into the milk, which makes it a little easier for them to participate.

**Kid-Friendly Explanation**

Milk contains water and fat.
When you add dishwashing liquid to the milk, the dishwashing liquid tries really, really hard to join up with the fats in the milk (hence why you need to use full fat milk). As it is racing towards the fat, it pushes everything else aside, including the food colouring, which is the reaction we see.

**What you need...**

- Full cream milk
- Food colouring
- Dishwashing liquid

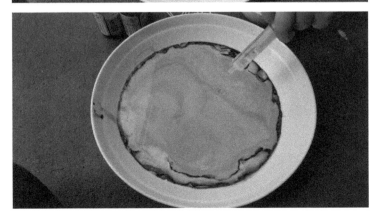

# STRING PHONES

*Poke a hole in the end of two tin cans with a nail and hammer, tie a piece of string between the two, hold them taut and have a good ole conversation.*

## Handy Hint

Experiment with holding the string very loosely versus tightly. What happens?
How about if a third person holds the centre of the string?
How far can you make the phone work?

## What you need...

- Hammer and nail (or toothpick for disposable cup)
- String
- 2 tin cans or even disposable cups work well

## Kid-Friendly Explanation

The air around us is made of tiny particles. Sound is made when the air particles vibrate and bump into each other. When you talk into the cup, the noise that you make vibrates the bottom of the cup, travels along the string, vibrating the string, and then travels into the other cup where the other person can hear it (the sound vibrates into their ear).

When the string goes slack, the sound can 'fall off'. When someone holds the string, it stops the string from vibrating, stopping the sound from reaching the other person.

**Note: Please ensure tin edges are smooth prior to use.**

# SINK OR FLOAT?

*Simply set up a bowl of water, grab some objects from around the home and explore what sinks and what floats.*

**Handy Hint**

Be sure to discuss with your child what they think will happen before you try this out.
A good range of objects to include in the experiment are rocks, bottle tops, pegs, a feather, a leaf, a coin, a shell, plastic straw, soap or an icy pole stick. But the most interesting one is an orange. Try it with the skin on, then with the skin off.

**Kid-Friendly Explanation**

At the preschool level, it is difficult to explain buoyancy and density. I simply explain that all objects are made of very, very small particles. In some objects, these particles are packed closer together than in others, which makes them denser. Denser items sink in water whereas less dense items float (it's not about size!) In the case of the orange, the skin contains a whole heap of tiny air pockets. When the skin is taken off, this actually makes the orange denser to a point where it sinks.

**Note: Please maintain constant supervision of young children around water.**

**What you need...**

- Small bowl of water
- Assortment of objects that will both sink and float

# CATAPULT

*Build a catapult from a cardboard tube and wooden spoon
and let loose.*

### Kid-Friendly Explanation

When you push down on the wooden spoon handle, this causes the other end of
the spoon to fly up and launch your paper in the air.

(There are a number of other catapults that you can build with elastic bands to
have a discussion around stored and kinetic energy, but for my preschooler, I
found that a simple explanation of cause and effect was enough).

**What you need...**

- Wooden spoon
- Cardboard tube
- Paper
- String

### Handy Hint

Explore different (soft) materials to see what goes farther or higher. You could even experiment with how long
the spoon is by replacing it with something different.

# SPONGE POWER BOAT

*Cut the front of the sponge to a point, cut a hole in the middle of the sponge then thread the balloon through. Insert a small length of tube in the balloon, blow it up and watch it move.*

**Handy Hint**

OK, so there are a few little tricks to this one. Firstly, make sure that the hole in the sponge is located approximately in the middle of the sponge.

Secondly, you need a way to direct the escaping air to the rear of the boat so that it moves forward. (If you just poke the balloon through, then the escaping air is located in the middle of the boat and it just keeps circulating on the one spot.) I used a small section of plastic pipe and inserted it into the balloon opening. I then taped it to the underside of the sponge so that it pointed directly backwards.

Oh, and if the boat is going a little too fast for you, just cut a small section of sponge from the offcuts and lodge it loosely in the pipe. The air will still keep coming out and power the boat, but at a slower pace.

**Kid-Friendly Explanation**

There is air in the balloon, and when you let go of the neck, the air escapes through the tube. The air that is escaping is pushing on the water behind the boat and therefore propels the boat forward. To demonstrate this, you could push yourself (i.e., the boat) off a wall (i.e., the water) with your hand (i.e., the stream of air).

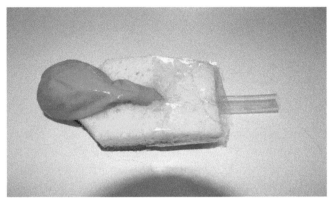

**What you need...**

- Balloon
- Sponge (thick is good)
- Bath (or paddling pool or other container big enough)
- A small length of plastic tube

# BALLOON ROCKETS AND CARS

*For this activity, all you really need to do is tie a piece of fishing line or string between two chairs, but be sure to place a straw on the string first! Then blow up a balloon and hold it shut whilst you tape it onto the straw. Let it go and watch the balloon fly!*

## Handy Hint

Got a car nut? We taped our balloon to a toy car and watched it fly! To do this you need to apply a piece of tape on the underside of the balloon and under the car as pictured.

If you find the air escaping too fast in kids fingers, peg the neck of the balloon so you can position it and let it go easily.

## Kid-Friendly Explanation

When you let go of the neck of the balloon, a stream of air escapes from the balloon causing 'thrust'; more simply, it propels the balloon forward. This is the same thing that happens in jet planes. Or in the swimming pool when you kick your feet and propel yourself forward.

**What you need...**
- Balloon
- Straw
- Smooth string or fishing line (you don't want too much friction)

# PULLEY ME UP

*Connect a piece of rope to a ½ full milk carton. Create a a pulley with a stick through a spool and secure it. Lift up the carton with the rope normally, and then lift it up by using the pulley; which is easier?*

**Handy Hint**

There are so many variations to this. You can try to connect a number of pulleys in a row and explore how much easier it is to lift the same load with more pulleys.

In a slight variation, my children made a lifting machine. They lifted a cup with a rolling pin over the edge of the staircase. This activity can be done over the edge of the table, but we like to do it over the edge of the stairs because if little fingers let go of the rolling pin it will simply be trapped between banisters.

We spent quite a bit of time transferring our Lego from the ground to the stairs via the lifting machine.

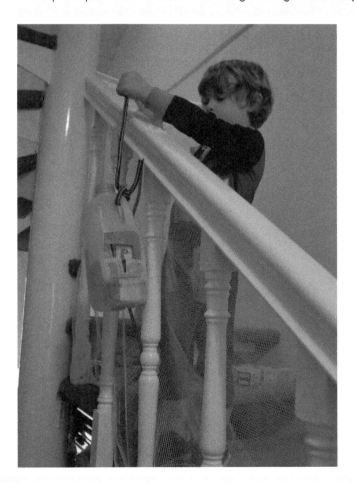

**What you need...**

-Stick
- Spool
- String
- Milk carton

**Kid-Friendly Explanation**

It is hard to lift heavy objects; it takes a lot of effort to lift a big load (weight of object).

When you use a pulley you pull down rather than pull up. It is easier to pull down (i.e., the same direction as gravity) than it is to pull up, so you can lift a load more easily this way.

# MAGNETISM

2 – 5 years

*Much like the magnetic sensory bottles (refer to page 51), pop some paper clips into a bottle filled with baby oil (to prevent rust), and use a magnet on the outside to explore what happens.*

**Handy Hint**

Of course, you don't actually need to make a magnetic bottle. I sent my son around the house with a magnet to explore and report back to me on what items stuck to the magnet.

**Kid-Friendly Explanation**

At this stage, electrons are beyond my 4 year old's understanding. So I have settled for saying that everything is made up of tiny particles, and sometimes these tiny particles create a force that we can't see, which is called magnetism. What magnetism does it that it pulls metal objects towards them. Magnets have opposite ends, so one end will pull metal towards it and the other will push metal items away from it.

**What you need...**

- Bottle
- Magnet
- Paper clips
- Baby oil (or water if it is not going to be kept a long time)

# WAVES

2 – 5 years

*Fill a large tub with water and blow on the surface of the water to observe the creation of waves.*

**Kid-Friendly Explanation**

When wind travels across the surface of the water, it pushes onto the water and transfers energy into the water, which creates waves.

**What you need...**

- Tub of water

**Handy Hint**

For older children, you can add a small object in the water and observe what happens when the wave passes through. Yes, the object moves up and down, but it does not move with the wave. Waves are energy being transferred between water particles, not those same particles moving through water (much like one marble hitting another and so forth).

**Note: Please maintain constant supervision of young children around water.**

# INDEX OF ACTIVITIES

| ACTIVITY | 0-6 MTHS | 6-12 MTHS | 1-2 YRS | 2-3 YRS | 3-5 YRS | GROSS MOTOR SKILLS | FINE MOTOR SKILLS | MESSY PLAY | QUIET PLAY | IMAGIN- ATIVE | STEM | PROBLEM SOLVING | SENSORY | PAGE |
|---|---|---|---|---|---|---|---|---|---|---|---|---|---|---|
| 3-LEGGED RACE | | | | | ✓ | ✓ | | | | | | | | 154 |
| A-MAZE-ING | | | | | ✓ | | | | | | | ✓ | | 116 |
| ACTIVE ALPHABET | | | ✓ | ✓ | ✓ | ✓ | | | | | | | | 151 |
| ACTIVITY JAR | | | ✓ | ✓ | ✓ | ✓ | | | | | | | | 99 |
| AIR BALL | | | ✓ | ✓ | ✓ | ✓ | | | | | | ✓ | | 90 |
| AIRPORT AND CARPARK | | | | ✓ | ✓ | | ✓ | | ✓ | ✓ | | | | 133 |
| ALPHABET THROW | | | | | ✓ | ✓ | | | ✓ | | | | | 149 |
| ANIMAL CHARADES | | | | ✓ | ✓ | | | | ✓ | ✓ | | | | 139 |
| ANIMAL WASHING STATION | | | ✓ | ✓ | ✓ | | | ✓ | ✓ | | | | | 74 |
| BABY JUG EXPLORATION | | | ✓ | | | | ✓ | | ✓ | | | ✓ | | 43 |
| BABY LAVA LAMPS | | | ✓ | ✓ | ✓ | | | | ✓ | | ✓ | | | 186 |
| BABY MAZE | | ✓ | | | | ✓ | | | ✓ | | | | | 60 |
| BALL CATCH | | | | | ✓ | ✓ | | | | | | | | 150 |
| BALL MAZE | | | | | ✓ | ✓ | | | | | | ✓ | | 167 |
| BALL TOSS | | | ✓ | ✓ | ✓ | ✓ | | | | | | | | 64 |
| BALLOON GAMES – ADVANCED | | | | | ✓ | ✓ | | | | | | | | 112 |
| BALLOON GAMES – BASIC | | | ✓ | ✓ | | ✓ | | | | | | | | 96 |
| BALLOON ROCKETS AND CARS | | | | | ✓ | | ✓ | | | | ✓ | ✓ | | 196 |
| BALLOONING | | | | ✓ | ✓ | | ✓ | | | | ✓ | | | 190 |
| BANDED TUBE | | | ✓ | | | | ✓ | | ✓ | | | ✓ | | 108 |
| BATHROOM FUN | | ✓ | ✓ | | | | | | | | | ✓ | ✓ | 54 |
| BATHROOM PAINTING | | | ✓ | ✓ | | | | ✓ | ✓ | | | | | 77 |
| BEAN SCOOP | | | | ✓ | ✓ | | | ✓ | | | | ✓ | ✓ | 148 |
| BOWLING | | | ✓ | ✓ | ✓ | ✓ | | | | | | | | 65 |
| BUBBLE BUBBLE | ✓ | | | | ✓ | | | | | | ✓ | | | 180 |
| BUBBLES BUBBLES BUBBLES | | | ✓ | ✓ | ✓ | | | ✓ | | | | | ✓ | 36 |
| BUILD YOUR OWN TRACK | | | ✓ | ✓ | ✓ | ✓ | | | ✓ | ✓ | | | | 110 |
| BUILDING BLOCKS | | | ✓ | ✓ | ✓ | | ✓ | | ✓ | | | ✓ | | 80 |
| CAR GARAGE | | | | ✓ | ✓ | ✓ | | | ✓ | ✓ | | | | 138 |
| CAR LAUNCHER | | | | | ✓ | | ✓ | | ✓ | | ✓ | ✓ | | 157 |
| CAR RAMPS | | | ✓ | ✓ | ✓ | | ✓ | | | | ✓ | ✓ | | 79 |
| CARDBOARD TUBE CRAFTS | | | | ✓ | ✓ | | ✓ | | ✓ | | ✓ | ✓ | | 127 |
| CATAPULT | | | | ✓ | ✓ | | ✓ | | | | ✓ | ✓ | | 194 |
| CLAY PLAY | | ✓ | ✓ | ✓ | ✓ | | ✓ | ✓ | ✓ | | | | ✓ | 70 |
| COLANDER THREAD | | | ✓ | ✓ | ✓ | | ✓ | | ✓ | | | ✓ | | 132 |
| COLOUR WHEEL | | | | ✓ | ✓ | | | ✓ | ✓ | | ✓ | | | 93 |
| COLOURING ON WINDOWS | | | ✓ | ✓ | ✓ | | | | ✓ | | ✓ | | | 82 |
| CONSTRUCTION SITE ANTICS | | | ✓ | ✓ | ✓ | | | ✓ | ✓ | ✓ | | ✓ | ✓ | 76 |
| COTTON BALL RACE | | | | ✓ | ✓ | ✓ | | | ✓ | | | | | 109 |
| COUNTRY IN A BOX | | | ✓ | ✓ | | | | | ✓ | | | | | 135 |
| CRUNCHY CONSTRUCTION | | | ✓ | ✓ | | ✓ | | ✓ | | | | | ✓ | 105 |
| CUP AND SPOONS | | ✓ | ✓ | ✓ | | | ✓ | | ✓ | | | ✓ | | 56 |

| ACTIVITY | AGE RANGE | | | | | ACTIVITY TYPE | | | | | | | | PAGE |
|---|---|---|---|---|---|---|---|---|---|---|---|---|---|---|
| | 0-6 MTHS | 6-12 MTHS | 1-2 YRS | 2-3 YRS | 3-5 YRS | GROSS MOTOR SKILLS | FINE MOTOR SKILLS | MESSY PLAY | QUIET PLAY | IMAGIN-ATIVE | STEM | PROBLEM SOLVING | SENSORY | |
| DANCE PARTY | ✓ | | | ✓ | ✓ | ✓ | | | | | | | | 68 |
| DANCING RIBBONS | ✓ | | ✓ | ✓ | | | | | | | | | ✓ | 29 |
| DANGLING NOISE | | ✓ | | | | | | | | | | | ✓ | 30 |
| DISCOVERY BOX | | | ✓ | | | | | | ✓ | | | | ✓ | 46 |
| DIY HANGING MOBILE | ✓ | | ✓ | | | | | | | | | | ✓ | 27 |
| DRUMS AND OTHER INSTRUMENTS | | ✓ | ✓ | | | | | | | | | | ✓ | 41 |
| ENGINEERING BRIDGES | | | | ✓ | | | ✓ | | ✓ | | ✓ | ✓ | | 175 |
| EXPERIMENTING WITH AIR | | | | | ✓ | | | | | | ✓ | ✓ | | 174 |
| FAMILY FUN | | ✓ | ✓ | | | | | | ✓ | | | | | 53 |
| FILL THE CUP | | | | ✓ | ✓ | | | | | | ✓ | | | 189 |
| FINGER PAINTING | | ✓ | ✓ | ✓ | ✓ | | | ✓ | | | | | ✓ | 35 |
| FINGER PUPPETS | ✓ | | | | | | | | ✓ | | | | ✓ | 23 |
| FIREWORKS | | | | | ✓ | | | | | | ✓ | | | 181 |
| FLYING SAUCERS | | | | ✓ | ✓ | ✓ | ✓ | | | | | | | 71 |
| FREEING THE ANIMALS | | | | ✓ | ✓ | | | | ✓ | | | ✓ | | 141 |
| GEOGRAPHY IN A BOX | | | | ✓ | ✓ | | | | ✓ | | | | ✓ | 134 |
| GROSS MOTOR SKILLS | | | ✓ | ✓ | ✓ | | ✓ | ✓ | | | | | | 101 |
| HIDE AND SEEK | | | ✓ | ✓ | ✓ | ✓ | | | | | | | | 89 |
| HIDE THE TOY | | ✓ | | | | | | | | | | | | 33 |
| HOT AND COLD AIR | | | | | ✓ | | | | | | ✓ | ✓ | | 182 |
| I SPY BOTTLE | | | ✓ | ✓ | ✓ | | | | ✓ | | | | ✓ | 91 |
| ICE CUBE SORT | | | ✓ | ✓ | ✓ | | ✓ | | ✓ | | | ✓ | | 100 |
| ICE HOCKEY | | | | ✓ | ✓ | | ✓ | | | | | | | 137 |
| ICYPOLE WEAVE | | | | | ✓ | | | | ✓ | | | ✓ | ✓ | 160 |
| IN THE SPOTLIGHT | | ✓ | ✓ | | | | | | | | | ✓ | ✓ | 58 |
| INDOOR CAMPING | | | ✓ | ✓ | ✓ | | | | ✓ | ✓ | | | | 87 |
| INDOOR CROQUET | | | | ✓ | ✓ | | ✓ | | | | | | | 113 |
| JUMPING JACK | | | | ✓ | ✓ | ✓ | | | | | | | | 111 |
| JUNIOR SCAVENGER HUNTS | | | | | ✓ | | | | | | | ✓ | | 62 |
| MAGNET SORTING | | ✓ | ✓ | | | | | | ✓ | ✓ | | | | 37 |
| MAGNETIC EXPLORATION | | | | ✓ | ✓ | | ✓ | | ✓ | | ✓ | | | 129 |
| MAGNETISM | | | | ✓ | ✓ | | ✓ | | | | ✓ | ✓ | | 198 |
| MARBLE TRACK RACES | | | | | ✓ | | ✓ | | | ✓ | | | | 156 |
| MATCHING GAME | | | ✓ | ✓ | ✓ | | ✓ | | ✓ | | | ✓ | | 84 |
| MEMORISATION | | | | ✓ | ✓ | | | | | | | ✓ | | 166 |
| MILK JUG TOSS | | | | ✓ | ✓ | ✓ | | | ✓ | | | ✓ | | 140 |
| MILK PLASTIC | | | ✓ | ✓ | ✓ | | ✓ | | | | ✓ | | ✓ | 75 |
| MINI GOLF | | | | ✓ | ✓ | ✓ | | | | | | | | 117 |
| MIRROR, MIRROR ON THE WALL | | | ✓ | ✓ | ✓ | ✓ | | | ✓ | ✓ | | ✓ | | 94 |
| MISSION IMPOSSIBLE | | | | | ✓ | ✓ | | | | | | ✓ | | 158 |
| MOUNTAIN CLIMBING | | ✓ | ✓ | ✓ | | ✓ | | | | | | | | 55 |
| MOUNTAINS | | | | | ✓ | | | | | | ✓ | | | 187 |

| ACTIVITY | 0-6 MTHS | 6-12 MTHS | 1-2 YRS | 2-3 YRS | 3-5 YRS | GROSS MOTOR SKILLS | FINE MOTOR SKILLS | MESSY PLAY | QUIET PLAY | IMAGINATIVE | STEM | PROBLEM SOLVING | SENSORY | PAGE |
|---|---|---|---|---|---|---|---|---|---|---|---|---|---|---|
| SOAP RACES | | | | ✓ | ✓ | ✓ | | ✓ | | | ✓ | ✓ | | 125 |
| SOCCER | | | ✓ | ✓ | ✓ | ✓ | | | | | | ✓ | | 66 |
| SOCK MATCHING GAME | | | ✓ | ✓ | | ✓ | ✓ | | | | | ✓ | | 103 |
| SPAGHETTI MADNESS | | ✓ | ✓ | ✓ | | | ✓ | ✓ | ✓ | | | | ✓ | 38 |
| SPIDERWEB TARGETS | | | | ✓ | ✓ | ✓ | | | ✓ | | | | | 128 |
| SPONGE BALLS | | | | ✓ | ✓ | | ✓ | ✓ | | | | | ✓ | 143 |
| SPONGE POWER BOAT | | | | | ✓ | | ✓ | | | | ✓ | ✓ | | 195 |
| SPONGE TOWER | | | ✓ | ✓ | | | ✓ | | ✓ | | | ✓ | | 88 |
| STACKING BLOCKS | | | ✓ | ✓ | | | | | ✓ | | | ✓ | | 106 |
| STACKING RINGS | | ✓ | ✓ | ✓ | | ✓ | ✓ | | ✓ | | | ✓ | | 61 |
| STAINED GLASS WINDOWS | | | ✓ | ✓ | ✓ | | ✓ | | ✓ | | | | | 78 |
| STATIC BUTTERFLY | | | | | ✓ | | ✓ | | ✓ | | ✓ | ✓ | | 183 |
| STICKY BALL CHALLENGE | | | ✓ | ✓ | | | ✓ | | ✓ | | | | | 104 |
| STOCKING FUN | | | | ✓ | ✓ | | | | ✓ | | | | | 102 |
| STRAW BUILDINGS | | | | | ✓ | | ✓ | | ✓ | | ✓ | ✓ | | 155 |
| STRAW ROCKETS | | | | | ✓ | | | | ✓ | | ✓ | ✓ | | 172 |
| STRING PHONES | | | | | ✓ | | | | | ✓ | ✓ | ✓ | | 192 |
| SUMO DUDES | | | | | ✓ | ✓ | | | | | | | | 161 |
| SWIRLY MILK | | | | ✓ | ✓ | | | | | | ✓ | | ✓ | 191 |
| TABLE BALL | | | | ✓ | ✓ | ✓ | | | | | ✓ | ✓ | | 162 |
| TACTILE TICKLES | ✓ | | | | | | | | | | | | ✓ | 28 |
| TARGET PRACTICE | | | ✓ | ✓ | ✓ | ✓ | | | | ✓ | | ✓ | | 144 |
| TEDDY BEAR'S PICNIC | | ✓ | ✓ | ✓ | ✓ | ✓ | | | ✓ | | | | ✓ | 69 |
| THAT'S A WRAP | | ✓ | ✓ | ✓ | ✓ | ✓ | ✓ | | ✓ | | | ✓ | | 59 |
| THE FLOWER FOOD | | | | ✓ | | ✓ | | | | | ✓ | ✓ | | 188 |
| TODDLER BALANCE BEAM | | | ✓ | ✓ | | | | | | | | | | 98 |
| TODDLER PUZZLES | | | | ✓ | ✓ | | | | ✓ | | | ✓ | | 145 |
| TORNADO IN A BOTTLE | | | | ✓ | ✓ | | | | ✓ | | ✓ | | ✓ | 177 |
| TOY FLYING FOX | | | | ✓ | ✓ | | | | ✓ | | ✓ | ✓ | | 159 |
| TREASURE CHEST | | | ✓ | ✓ | | | ✓ | | ✓ | ✓ | | | ✓ | 83 |
| TUNNEL | | ✓ | ✓ | ✓ | | ✓ | | | ✓ | | | | ✓ | 49 |
| TWINKLE TWINKLE LITTLE STAR | ✓ | | | | | | | | ✓ | | | | ✓ | 22 |
| UP UP AND AWAY | ✓ | | | | | | | | ✓ | | | | | 25 |
| VEGETABLE STAMPS | | ✓ | ✓ | ✓ | ✓ | ✓ | ✓ | ✓ | | | | ✓ | ✓ | 48 |
| VOLCANOES | | | | ✓ | ✓ | | | ✓ | | | ✓ | ✓ | | 179 |
| WATER LIFECYCLE | | | | ✓ | ✓ | | | | | | ✓ | | | 176 |
| WATER PLAY - ADVANCED | | ✓ | | ✓ | ✓ | | ✓ | ✓ | | | ✓ | ✓ | ✓ | 122 |
| WATER PLAY - BASIC | | | ✓ | ✓ | | ✓ | ✓ | ✓ | | | ✓ | ✓ | ✓ | 42 |
| WAVES | | | | ✓ | ✓ | ✓ | | ✓ | | ✓ | ✓ | | | 199 |
| WE'RE GOING ON A BEAR HUNT | | ✓ | ✓ | | | | | | ✓ | ✓ | | | | 120 |
| WEB RESCUE | | | | ✓ | ✓ | | | | ✓ | ✓ | | ✓ | | 163 |